LOST
SHADOW

Song Dog Adventures

Street Shadows
Lost Shadow

LOST SHADOW

A Song Dog Adventure

Claire Gilchrist

DUNDURN
PRESS

Publisher: Scott Fraser | Acquiring editor: Kathryn Lane | Editor: Susan Fitzgerald
Cover designer: Laura Boyle
Cover image: landscape: istock.com/ok-sana; coyotes: shutterstock.com/Sloth Astronaut
Printer: Marquis Book Printing Inc.

Library and Archives Canada Cataloguing in Publication

Title: Lost shadow / Claire Gilchrist.
Names: Gilchrist, Claire, 1983- author.
Description: Series statement: A song dog adventure | Sequel to: Street shadows.
Identifiers: Canadiana (print) 20210205679 | Canadiana (ebook) 20210205695 | ISBN 9781459748255 (softcover) | ISBN 9781459748262 (PDF) | ISBN 9781459748279 (EPUB)
Classification: LCC PS8613.I41 L68 2021 | DDC jC813/.6—dc23

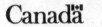
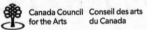

We acknowledge the support of the Canada Council for the Arts and the Ontario Arts Council for our publishing program. We also acknowledge the financial support of the Government of Ontario, through the Ontario Book Publishing Tax Credit and Ontario Creates, and the Government of Canada.

Dundurn Press
1382 Queen Street East
Toronto, Ontario, Canada M4L 1C9
dundurn.com, @dundurnpress 𝕏 f ⌾

We can be ethical only in relation to something we can see, feel, understand, love, or otherwise have faith in.

— Aldo Leopold, *A Sand County Almanac*

PART ONE
PICA AND SCRUFF

ONE
FOREST

Pica

Pica woke from her nap and, without opening her eyes, curled up more tightly against Scruff. The warmth from his body helped ward off the cold radiating up from the frozen ground. From the nearby street, car horns shouted at each other, and tires squished along in the rain. *Ugh. Winter.* Although it was only her first winter, she was already sure that it was her least favourite season.

A little while later, after a particularly loud truck horn honked, Scruff stirred. She felt him lift his head, and then, a few seconds later, he thumped it back down onto the hard-packed dirt.

"Do you feel it?" he asked quietly.

"Feel what?" Pica cracked one eye and squinted at him, puzzled.

"The sun."

Pica opened both eyes wider and looked through a gap in the branches of the bush where they lay. All she could see was grey sky. She could hear the rain pounding the ground around them, and freezing drops seeped through the dense cover, dropping onto her already soaking fur.

"Ha. Right. Now you're going crazy on me."

"No, really. Just close your eyes and think about it. It's the hillside. You're lying in the long grass, with the crickets chirping. You can smell the earth baking in the heat. Your fur feels hot, but you're too lazy to move. You can sense the sun behind your eyelids, so bright and warm." He paused, and suddenly, Pica saw it all.

The hillside above the golf course was where she and her three siblings were raised. It was a paradise: long, hot days and long, soft grasses. Her first few months had been perfect, together with her whole family, learning how to hunt and playing with her older brother, Dane. Perfect — until Scruff and Jagger had come and ruined everything. She breathed in sharply, remembering the day that her father had not come home. She knew now that Scruff had been tricked into helping kill her father, manipulated by his older brother, Jagger. But at the time, rage had burned white-hot in her body.

Another loud car horn brought her back to the present. She lifted her head to look over at Scruff, softening as she reflected on how much had changed since that day. His eyes were closed, and he had a goofy smile on his face. They had teamed up to fight off Jagger and then travelled to the Wild Lands for a new life. It was time to move on and put the past where it belonged: in the past.

She jumped up and shook her wet fur in his face, smiling as his eyes popped open and he frowned.

"Hey, you ruined my nap in the sun!"

"I'm hungry. Dreaming about the past is not going to help us survive this winter."

"I'm hungry, too." He gave her chin a little lick. "I'm just trying to make us feel better."

Pica sighed. "I know. Thank you. But we're never going back to the golf course. It's not even a golf course anymore, with all the houses the humans have built on it. This is our life now, and it's winter. Let's figure out where to find food today."

She gently touched his nose to soften her speech. Weeks ago, they had crossed the bridge to these Wild Lands in search of a new home. But since then, they hadn't found any good territory that wasn't already occupied by a coyote pack, and they hadn't found much food, either. They had hoped for more opportunity here, because the houses were farther apart, and there were more green spaces. Being young, small coyotes unable to challenge larger coyotes for territory, what they needed was to find somewhere less competitive to start their new life together. Unfortunately, it seemed they weren't the first to discover this area; there were just as many big coyotes fighting for a good territory here as there were in the city. At this point, they were starting to feel trapped. Going back to the city wasn't a solution, but they weren't sure they could find a home here, either.

Pica's stomach growled loudly, and Scruff poked her with his nose. "I heard that. That's enough moping for both of us. It's time to go meet the local mice!"

She found herself smiling despite her hunger and the cold. It was hard, but being with Scruff made it better. He made everything fun. That was what she had liked about him the first time she met him, when he had appeared at the golf course one day, wanting to chase a ball down the hill with her. He'd always been able to cheer her up. She jumped up and shook some of the water off her fur, feeling a tiny glimmer of joy. Even though things were bad, at least she had her best friend by her side.

They spent the next half hour cleaning and grooming themselves carefully, licking the water off their fur and getting the dirt out from between the pads of their feet. It was an evening ritual they had started while waiting for it to get dark enough to head out safely. Finally, the sky darkened, and the world around them faded to shades of grey.

As they left the undesirable area full of smelly, scrubby bushes where they had been forced to spend the day, Pica looked at Scruff thoughtfully. "I think we should try something new tonight."

Scruff cocked his head to the side. "What? You don't want to wander around in the rain all night and be cold and wet and get chased by other coyotes? Why not?"

Pica shook her head, laughing. "Scruff. Be serious. We clearly aren't having much luck in this area. We need to get farther away from humans and territory that's already been claimed. I think we need to head deeper into the forest and —"

"No."

She glared at him. "Let me finish. We should head deeper into the big forest and see what it's like. Maybe we'll be able to find our own hunting grounds there."

"We've already talked about it. It's too great a risk."

She thought about their third day in the Wild Lands. They had been so full of anticipation then, certain they were about to discover something magical. On the edge of a housing development, they had found a deep, dark forest with trees bigger than any she'd ever seen before. They hadn't been able to hear or smell an end to it. Curious, they had ventured in, and within five minutes were confronted with a set of smells and sounds they never experienced in the city. They smelled lots of birds and rodents, but puzzlingly, they didn't come across a single coyote marking. They had tripped over each other with joy. Maybe this would be a good place to make a home.

But then they had smelled something strange. Pica hadn't recognized it, but something in the way her body reacted told her it was dangerous. The fur had stood up on the back of her neck, and, looking over at Scruff, she'd seen his fur standing up, too. Whatever it was, it felt bigger and darker than anything they had ever encountered in the city. Without discussion, they had both turned around and fled the forest. They had never returned.

"Listen." Pica sighed now. "It might be dangerous, but there is risk here, too. We aren't finding enough mice, and if we eat another bad batch of human garbage, we might get too weak to hunt. I'm not saying we'll go forever. I just think we need to investigate a little bit more."

Scruff hesitated. Then his stomach gave a loud rumble. He smiled ruefully. "All right. My stomach agrees with you. We'll go in, but not far. Just enough to find out more about the forest. And if we see any coyotes nearby, we'll ask them about it. And if we smell that … thing, we get out."

"Deal." Pica smiled. For the first time this week, she felt a small puff of hope rising inside of her. Finally, they were taking action. The forest could be great for them, and even if it wasn't, how much worse could it be than what they were already experiencing?

TWO
CAT

Pica

Pica followed Scruff as he carefully wound his way around the houses, heading uphill toward the big forest. Although Pica's muscles felt slow and heavy from the cold and hunger, as they moved, she began to limber up. They took a few detours to avoid other coyote territories, but they made steady progress. As the pair climbed the hill, they encountered fewer and fewer houses, and the forest began to take over. This area was especially popular with coyotes, because it didn't have the menace of the deep forest but was still very quiet and peaceful. They stayed alert for signs of danger; because they were small and young, they couldn't risk a confrontation. Following a dry streambed that served as the neutral coyote path through the neighbourhood, they passed dark house after dark house.

Smelling a territory boundary, they detoured up the stream bank to the backyard of a house, planning to cut a wide arc in order to avoid the other coyote. The house was quiet and mostly dark, with only a few lights shining on the top floor.

Pica was sniffing around the back of the house, looking for food, when Scruff yelped. "Hey, it's a beach!" he called. She turned to see him bouncing around in a big box filled with sand.

Pica trotted over and delicately dipped her paw in. The sand was cold, and it stuck between her toe pads. She looked around. There was no sign of water. "Some beach."

"It's nice, I think." Scruff flopped down, then immediately jumped up again, as if something had bitten him. "Well, it would be nice, if it wasn't so freezing cold out."

"Hey, check it out." Pica gestured toward the house. A light flickered on downstairs, illuminating the silhouette of a person in the window. Two smaller figures ran through the room, yelling. Pica jumped as the back door suddenly clicked open. "Freeze!" she whispered to Scruff.

A man walked out with a bag in his hand. He yelled something back through the door before closing it, the sound ringing loudly in the air and making Pica's heart race. He headed straight toward them, holding the bag high over his head to block the rain. Walking quickly past the sandbox, he didn't notice them. Pica followed him with her eyes, keeping the rest of her body perfectly still, a shadow in the darkness. As the man disappeared out the back gate, she wondered how humans could be so powerful when their senses seemed so weak.

Her eyes flickered toward a new sound coming from the house. The door clicked open again, and a tiny shape peered out. A small child ran into the yard, following the man's path. Her chubby legs took quick, unsteady steps. Just as she was passing the sandbox, she stopped, turning her head. Pica found herself looking straight into the girl's eyes.

"Ah!" the child shouted, gleefully pointing at her.

Pica jumped, surprised at the loud sound. Before she could process what was happening, the man's footsteps sounded as he returned from the other side of the back gate. Pica went numb, and she leapt out of the sandbox, fleeing the yard. She could sense Scruff behind her.

Only when they were a few blocks away did her body begin to calm. She turned to Scruff. "Can you believe it? Humans are so weird. It's like the little ones are smarter than the big ones. That little one definitely saw us."

"I know! The big one wasn't much of a threat, huh?"

She glanced sharply at him, noticing his confident tone. "Humans don't always show us their power," she reminded him.

"I don't know … that little one seemed pretty harmless, even when she saw you. Tiny little thing."

"I bet that tiny thing could kick your butt if she wanted to."

"Probably. I just wonder sometimes, you know? What the source of their power is. We've certainly never seen it."

Pica frowned and decided to change the subject. They were having this type of conversation more and more frequently, and she didn't want to argue right now. "All right, we're almost at the big forest. I can smell it now."

They picked a new path up the hill and finally reached the place where the houses ended and the biggest trees began.

"Scruff, check it out! The wild!" she cried joyfully over her shoulder, leading the way into the shadows of the forest. "I can smell the fat mice already. I'll race you in."

"Pica …"

"I know." She looked back at him and smiled. "Just kidding. We'll proceed with caution."

They found a narrow dirt path and padded softly uphill. It was darker in here, with the sky blocked out by the tree canopy. Tall ferns carpeted the ground. The noise of the city faded away, leaving only the sound of raindrops falling on the leaves and needles far above their heads. Pica began to warm up and relax. It was so nice to be out of the wind and protected from the rain. She picked her way carefully up a steep, rocky path.

They were both beginning to enjoy the quiet, soothing sounds of the forest when they heard the distinctive squeak of a squirrel. Without needing to communicate, they slowed down and split up. Pica's ears swivelled quickly back and forth, tracking the sounds carefully. There were two squirrels, and they were scratching around at the base of a large tree trunk. If she gave herself away, they would climb up the tree in a flash. She had to work with Scruff to take them by surprise.

Creeping forward slowly, she lifted her paws higher than normal and placed them down heel first, slowly rolling her weight forward, toward her toes. Scruff would be doing the same thing. The occasional rustle of leaves underfoot was muffled by the sound of the rain and the wind in the trees. Knowing Scruff was a few feet away, Pica made her big move. She circled the tree quickly and cut off the squirrels' path to the trunk, flushing them both toward Scruff. In a few seconds, it was done. Scruff had trapped one of them between his lightning-quick paws.

"Well done, Pica! That was beautiful!" rang Scruff's gleeful voice across the clearing.

Pica smiled. Despite the lack of food over the last few weeks, they had been steadily improving at hunting together. Due to an eye infection she had suffered as a pup, Pica's vision wasn't as good as Scruff's. They had worked out a hunting style where she chased the prey toward Scruff, and he trapped it with his paws.

They moved to a new area and began hunting again, their appetite now activated. Over the next few hours, they caught a few more rodents and found some plants and bark to eat. Pica's belly was full for the first time in weeks. She flopped down on a mossy rock.

"Break?" she suggested.

"I don't know …" Scruff looked around cautiously. "Should we just call it a win and get out of here while things are good?"

Pica sighed, looking down the hill. They were deep in the forest now, and the road seemed a long way off.

"Maybe. But I'm so tired. And it's warm in here. We can take turns staying awake to look out for danger."

"I don't know. It seems so strange to me that there aren't any other coyotes here."

"I know, it's weird. But we really need food and rest right now. Let's crawl underneath that log. I'll stay awake first."

Scruff reluctantly followed, crouching to join her in the hollow under a large mossy log. Pica sighed contentedly, rolling close to him to feel the heat coming off his fur. "I haven't felt this full and happy in a long time," she said sleepily. She realized that the rain had stopped. "This place is incredible."

Scruff turned his head to lick her. "Well, the first few hours here have been a success. Except when you tried to jump across that stream to catch that mouse ..."

"That was nothing compared to you falling off that rock!" It was easier to laugh about their hunting failures when they weren't hungry. Then they were both quiet, and Pica listened to the gentle wind in the trees. She watched the world carefully, until her eyes got too heavy and she joined Scruff in a deep sleep.

A loud series of thumps jolted Pica awake. She tried to jump to her feet, but hit her head on something. Where was she? She peeked out from under the log and remembered, realizing that they had slept for hours! The big thump came again, followed by a light rumble. The sounds were louder now. She cowered deeper under the log. Was this the thing they had feared?

"Don't move," hissed Scruff, flattening himself behind her.

They barely had time to take a breath before something large raced past the fallen log. There was a screech, and then another thing passed them. Wind hit her fur, ruffling it.

"What was —"

"Shh!"

They heard a third thing coming. Pica craned her head to see what it was this time as it whipped past. Just a human on a bike. Something they'd seen many times in the city. Scary, but not unknown.

They waited, frozen, to see if anything else would appear, but nothing did. It seemed as though quiet was restored to the forest.

"Whoa," Scruff breathed quietly. "I've never seen them going so fast before."

"Yes, and in the deep forest, too." Pica's mind spun. Were the humans chasing something? Was this connected to the source of their secret power?

"Were they running from something, do you think?" Scruff asked.

Pica's belly clenched. She hadn't thought about that possibility. "What would a human run from?"

"I don't want to find out." Scruff turned to her, his large golden eyes wide with worry.

"Me, neither. But it's weird that they left us alone."

"They probably just didn't see us. As usual." Scruff sounded impatient. "We should head back now."

"While we're still alive." She swallowed, considering their options. "Let's take our time, though, and find some more food."

"Sounds good to me, but let's not get too far apart. We're really alone out here, and I still feel like we're missing something."

They headed back down the hill. Pica swivelled her head to take it all in. It was morning now, and they could see more of what was around them. Huge tree trunks flanked the trail, the rough brown bark stretching up to the green forest canopy. The moss and ferns that coated the forest floor barely masked the tempting smells of small animals. Her stomach reminded her that she was hungry again. "I'm going to look for food down there by that stream on our way back."

Scruff made a move to follow her, but Pica stopped him. "I want to try on my own. There are so many mice here, I feel like I might actually have a shot at getting one without you. I'll just be right there — you can see me. Why don't you stay here and keep an eye out for beasts? Yelp if you see any danger, and I'll come right back."

Scruff looked at her for a moment before shaking his head. "Okay, fine. But don't go far. I'll be over there by that open rock area."

Pica picked her way down the hill toward the sound of water. When she reached the creek, she breathed in with delight at the water spilling over the large, smooth rocks. It was magical. Everything was alive and green. In the city, she had never been far from the sights and sounds of human life, not even on the golf course or in the city forests. Here, the deep forest blocked out human sounds completely, leaving only the humming rhythm of the plants and animals.

She dipped her head down to the water, drinking deeply. It was so cold that it hurt her throat. She stepped in, then jumped back when she felt its force. For a moment she watched the running water, hypnotized by the swirls and froth, then walked a little farther downhill, following the stream. She was focused on the smells of the rodents, but just as she gracefully stepped over a decaying log, her fur suddenly began to prickle. Something was there with her. Then she smelled it: a strong, musty stench. Was it the beast?

She whirled around, scanning the trees and swivelling her ears, hoping to pick up on something, anything, that could give her more information. Nothing — just the smell. Alert, she waited for a few minutes, her muscles tense. Still nothing. For a split second, she doubted herself. Was she overreacting, just nervous about being in such a new place?

She turned around to head back toward Scruff, walking carefully along a large log. Every sound made her skin crawl, and she kept whipping her head around to look behind her, sure there was something there. Then she did something she hadn't done since she had first sensed danger. She looked up above her head.

Two bright-yellow eyes stared at her from a branch right above her head. She gasped and froze, a jolt of adrenalin shooting through her body.

It looked like a cat, but it was much, much bigger than any cat she'd ever seen. It crouched on the branch, absolutely still, its large muscles well defined under golden fur. For a moment, they stared at each other. Then the cat's muscles twitched, and she knew instinctively that it was going to attack her.

"Scruff!" she yelped desperately. But he was too far away. Something white-hot raked her back, and a giant weight ground her body into the cold dirt. Her head slammed against a rock. In a daze, she curled up, trying to protect her stomach and throat. Strange claws sank into her side, and she realized with panic that she would not be able to fight off this beast.

THREE
BREAD

Scruff

The moment he heard the yelp, Scruff knew Pica was in deep trouble. He raced toward the cries of terror, giving a series of short barks to let her know he was coming. He had never heard her so desperate before. He cleared a fallen log and saw a large mass of yellow fur. Pica's terrified shrieks were coming from under it. As he slid to a halt, a large head emerged and turned to stare at him with two huge yellow eyes. Scruff's heart stopped. He was unsure of what to do next — the beast was at least five times his size.

Pica gasped for air. The sound activated something deep inside him, and a growl ripped out of his chest. He felt his fur stand up along his back. The beast stared at him a moment longer, then flicked its tail, turning and gliding into the forest in one fluid motion.

"Pica!" Scruff closed the gap in a single leap and crouched above her. Her eyes were closed, and she didn't respond. "Pica!" he called again, more insistent this time, and pushed his nose against her head. She groaned. He nosed along her body from top to bottom, looking for major wounds. He found blood coming out of deep cuts on her back and side, but none on her belly, where injuries would be much more dangerous.

Pica made a sound then and struggled to lift her head. Her eyes were open now. She breathed in and out slowly. "Did I just get beaten up by a ... cat?" Her voice was a croak.

Scruff blinked. "Are you joking?"

"You're right. It doesn't feel too funny." Pica's head hit the dirt again, and she groaned.

Scruff glanced around nervously. "I don't know what it was. It wasn't like any cat I've ever seen."

Pica gave a weak chuckle. "You can say that again. It was a monster cat."

"Monster cat." Scruff tried to smile, appreciating Pica's spirit. But this was exactly what he had feared. The forest contained things that were completely new and dangerous. He glanced around nervously, worried the cat might come back.

Pica's smile faded as she lifted her head again, struggling to look around, as well. "You were right. We can't stay here a minute longer. We'll never survive. Who knows what else is in this forest?"

They were both silent. The weight of disappointment was heavy.

Scruff licked her face gently. "Can you walk?"

"I sure hope so."

He watched her slowly roll onto her belly and push herself up onto her feet. She was a bit unsteady, but he saw the determination in her eyes and knew better than to comment. Together, they made their way downhill, keeping the dirt trail in sight. He couldn't shake the feeling that they were being followed, but he tried not to glance back, wanting Pica to focus on walking. He noticed with some relief that her legs seemed to be uninjured, and although there was blood matted in her fur, it didn't appear to be flowing.

They reached the edge of the forest, leaving the canopy of trees. Cold rain pelted them, mixing with Pica's dried blood to create a pink stream rolling off her fur. Scruff had to find somewhere safe for Pica, somewhere out of the rain. It had to be close by, both because Pica was exhausted, and because the daylight made travel much more dangerous.

Pica slumped on the pavement, waiting for him to take the lead. This was so uncharacteristic of her that Scruff felt a flash of concern. "I'm so sorry, Pica. I should have been there. Maybe the Wild Lands are just too much for us. Maybe you'd be better off with your family back in the city."

Pica suddenly came alive, whipping her head up to glare at him. "What are you talking about? This is not helpful. Just find a place for us to lie down. We can talk about it later."

"Okay." That was true — even if he was right, this wasn't the time or the place to discuss it. "Let's head down the hill and see what we can find."

It took them about an hour to locate a spot that would do. It wasn't much, just a small patch of scrubby grass and bushes underneath a power line. There wasn't much shelter from the rain, but no other coyotes who had marked it, and it was far enough away from the big forest that they could both relax a bit. There were houses and roads on either side, but the green space in the middle had few signs of human activity. It would have to do.

Pica immediately curled up in the bushes at the foot of a tree, and Scruff curled up beside her to keep her warm. He spent the first few hours carefully cleaning her wounds so she could begin to heal. As darkness came, she fell into a fitful sleep. Scruff stayed beside her, calming her each time she jolted awake in a panic. His thoughts drifted to their life in the city. She had been well cared for by her family. Would she want to go back now? Had the Wild Lands finally beaten them down? His stomach clenched thinking about it. Scruff had been involved in the killing of Pica's father. Even though he'd been tricked into it by Jagger, he knew he'd never be welcome in their pack. But he would understand if Pica wanted to go back, and if so, he'd help her get there. In the meantime, he'd have to find some food so she could get her strength back.

Scruff was alone with his thoughts throughout the long night, but finally the sky lightened, and so did the rain. As the birds began to chirp, a mouth-watering smell jolted him back to the present. He stood up, stretching.

Pica didn't wake. Her side was moving up and down with steady breathing. Good. He'd be back soon, hopefully with something good to eat.

He left the power lines and headed straight for the smell. Breaking through the bushes, he saw that the buildings on this side of the green space weren't actually houses. Down a short hill and across a road lay four low metal buildings surrounded by a big parking lot filled with trucks. He had seen buildings like these in the city, and there was usually good mouse hunting around them. But as the sweet smell wafted toward him again, all thoughts of mice left his head. His mouth watered.

The road was quiet, and he crossed it easily. It didn't take him long to find a hole in the wire fence. He soon found himself near the building with the strongest, sweetest smell. A truck was backed up against it, and a large metal door was open, allowing him to peek into the factory. There were big pallets everywhere, and the sound of humans. He slunk under the truck as footsteps approached.

Realizing he was taking a big risk, Scruff felt a little guilty. Normally, they never tried to get food when there were humans around. Pica especially was very cautious around humans. However, right now, she was in need of a good meal. And he was trapped now, anyway. Some humans walked out and began loading pallets onto the truck. The truck bed above his head shook under their heavy boots.

After a few minutes, the humans went back into the building, and everything was still. This was his chance.

He squeezed out from underneath the truck and stood tall, shaking out his coat and looking in every direction to make sure he was alone. Nothing moved. He jumped into the back of the truck and put his front paws up on one of the stacks. Bags of sweet-smelling food were lined up neatly from one end of the pallet to the other. He paused once more to look around and make sure no one was coming. Then he grabbed one of the packages with his teeth and fled, his heart pounding in his chest.

He raced across the parking lot and scrambled under the fence. As he did, the package got snagged on the wire and tore as he pulled to free it. The food — a large loaf of bread — spilled onto the ground. He abandoned the packaging and opened his jaws wide to grasp the loaf in his mouth. As he galloped across the road and up the hill to the power lines, the taste of the bread made his mouth water so badly that he could feel saliva dripping out the sides. He felt exhilarated, excited to be able to share it with Pica.

He approached her softly, carefully laying the loaf in front of her nose. Her eyes were closed, but when the smell of food began to saturate the air around them, her whiskers twitched, then her nose. She cracked an eye open.

"Am I dreaming?"

He smiled down at her. "Nope, check it out! Fresh and delicious."

"Really?" She shook her head, looking dazed.

"Help yourself."

She sniffed, and her eyes widened. She seemed to come to life. "Human food?" she said. "Where did you get this?"

Scruff hesitated, trying to evade the question. "There are some buildings on the other side of the road, just down there." He gestured with his head.

Pica narrowed her eyes. "Was it in the garbage?"

"Uh, sort of. Well, it was stacked up inside a truck. But don't worry, no one saw me."

"You went into a truck? In daylight?" Her tone was sharp.

Scruff felt a familiar anger welling up. He shook out his fur, breathing hard. "Let's not get into it right now. Just eat the food."

She shook her head. "What if something had happened to you? How would that have helped me? We've talked about this, Scruff. So many times. Humans are powerful."

He took a deep breath. "Come on, I won't do it again. But I already got it. Might as well eat it." He dipped his head and started gobbling up the bread. It was incredible, soft and sweet.

"No." Pica turned her back to him, curled herself up tightly, and put her head down.

Scruff stared at her. How could she be so stubborn? She needed this. "Eat it."

"No. You crossed the line. It's one thing to forage human garbage. But to go into a human truck? That's way too dangerous."

He swallowed his next bite. Something inside of him snapped.

"I know it was dangerous. But you know what else is dangerous? Being injured, without a home, in the middle

23

of winter. You aren't okay, Pica. We aren't okay. You need to eat this now to give yourself some strength. Then we can talk about a plan."

Pica twisted her head to glare at him as he continued to eat, slowing down now to savour the seeds sprinkled on top. He saw some drool escape the edge of her mouth. She was so stubborn.

Scruff pushed the last of the food toward her with his nose until it was right next to her face. He would make one more attempt. "We're not going to grow up to be self-sufficient if we die of starvation this winter. We both know you're not a great hunter at the best of times, and now that you're injured, we may need to relax our rules about human food for a few days."

Pica's body tensed, and her head whipped up, her eyes lasering his. "What did you say?"

Scruff stepped back, confused. "That we might need to —"

"That I'm not a good hunter."

He sighed. "You know what I mean."

"I do know what you mean. That you'd be better off without me dragging you down. I can't hunt well, and now I'm injured."

"No! Don't twist my words. We each have our own strengths, and we need to work together as a team." He growled, frustrated. "Don't be so proud."

His words hung in the air, heavy. They stared at each other, both breathing hard. Finally, Pica huffed, "I can't talk to you right now. Do what you want. See if I care." She walked stiffly away to another bush, then curled up and turned her head away from him. He sighed. He knew on some level that she was right — what he'd done this morning was the biggest risk he'd ever taken around humans. But at this moment, cold, hungry, and injured as she was, he wasn't sure why she was being so stubborn.

FOUR
TRUCK

Pica

Pica didn't sleep much that day. She was hungry, cold, and her wounds throbbed. Even worse, when she did nod off, she had disturbing dreams. In one, Scruff stood on top of a huge pile of human food, and when he noticed her, he glanced away, as if she were a small, insignificant bug. In another, the monster cat was attacking her, and she watched Scruff turn and walk away. Each time she woke with a start from a dream, the cold and the pain returned.

At the first sign of dusk, she stood and shook out her damp fur. She couldn't stop shivering. Her body ached. She didn't even feel hungry anymore, which she knew was a bad sign.

She glanced over at the bush where Scruff was curled up, asleep, his back to her. She felt a force pulling her toward him, but the memory of their fight was still fresh. His words, "you're not a great hunter at the best of times," rang repeatedly through her head. She had to clear it. She walked away quickly, taking stock of her injuries. All of the blood had dried, and her wounds stretched like tight elastic bands across her sides and her back. Her head pounded, and she felt as if her legs were disconnected from the rest of her body. After a minute of slow walking, she began to warm up slightly, and her thoughts turned to food.

She hunted with as much energy and focus as she could muster that night, but it was fruitless. She chased a couple of gophers and cornered a mouse but wasn't able to catch anything. She found a few scraps in human garbage cans, but not enough to help her regain her strength. As the night wore on, her anger gradually faded, replaced with deep weariness and shame. Scruff had only been trying to help her, and she really did need him right now.

She circled back to the power lines a few times to rest, but Scruff wasn't there. The small pile of human food was gone. She felt a wave of sadness and loneliness, and decided to lie down to wait for him. They would talk it out like they always did. The chill returned to her body, and she shivered for hours, waiting. When dawn broke, he still hadn't returned.

Her anxiety had increased while she waited. As the outlines of grey clouds became visible across the sky, she found herself standing again, walking in circles. Where was he? Was he still mad at her? A sweet smell wafted toward her from the buildings down the road, making her belly rumble, and a thought came to her. What if she went to get another loaf of bread to share with him when he got back? That way, she could show him that she understood how grim things were, and that she was willing to change, at least temporarily.

She walked cautiously toward the smell, crossing the road and pausing at the fence. Was she really going to do this? If she wanted to continue her life with Scruff, they were going to have to figure out a way to survive. And today, this would be the way. Her breath came in and out faster as she crouched down to squeeze between two sections of fence that had pulled apart slightly. The metal scraped against one of the wounds on her back, and she yelped. She quickly scanned the low buildings, hoping she hadn't alerted the humans. No one emerged.

She zeroed in on the source of the smell — the largest of the low, grey buildings — and crept closer, keeping low to the ground. She inhaled carefully, parsing the sweet food smells and the musty human smells, and swivelled her ears quickly, making sure that she didn't miss anything behind her. As she came around the side of the building, she froze. Three humans were standing in a circle, holding little sticks to their mouths. The acrid smell of smoke suddenly clogged her nostrils. If any one of them turned in her direction, they would see her. Her breath caught in her throat as she quickly ducked back around the corner.

A truck started up behind her, the roar vibrating her eardrums. Her path of retreat was cut off, unless she wanted to run past the truck. She sank down to the ground and froze, hoping no one looked in her direction. She didn't even twitch her whiskers.

She heard footsteps approaching and readied herself to flee, but then there was the sound of a door opening, and all three humans disappeared back into the building. Pica's chest rose and fell rapidly as she tried to stop her legs from shaking. She began to turn around slowly, but the shrill beeping of the truck behind her as it backed up cut off her avenue of escape. She leapt around the corner, past where the humans had been standing, and found herself face to face with another truck. This one wasn't running, though, and the back was open. She could see hulking piles of bread in pallets stacked as high as the top of the truck.

Although her urge to flee was strong, the smell was intoxicating. Taking a breath and checking again that the humans were gone, she ran up the steps into the back of the truck, her claws skittering on the cold metal floor. She grabbed one of the bags protruding from the middle of the first stack, tugging at it as she braced herself with her front paws. It wouldn't budge. She tried at the next stack. Same thing. The bags were protected by the edges of the pallet. How had Scruff gotten a package out? She scanned the interior of the truck quickly, trying to think. Then she spotted a shorter stack along the far side, with unprotected packages sitting on the very top pallet. That was it! She leapt over to it, wincing as her wounds stretched. Aware of the passing seconds, she reached up with her front paws and was just able to grab one of the topmost packages with her teeth. *Yes!*

Just then, the building door opened with a bang. She froze. The humans were back. A shadow fell across the opening of the truck, and before Pica could consider what to do, one of the humans pulled the truck door shut, plunging her into darkness. She hadn't even had time to take a breath — the bag of bread was still lodged between her jaws.

She let the package fall and leapt over to the door, pushing her nose up to the thin crack. Fresh air leaked in. She leaned against the door, testing it. It was solid. Her mind beginning to spin, she took a few steps back and flung herself against the door. Her body hit it with a thud, activating all of her bruises — the pain took her breath away.

She scanned the interior of the truck for another way out. Ignoring the aching in her body, she leapt from corner to corner, running her nose along the seams. Nothing. And then, the situation became infinitely worse: the truck roared to life. The cold metal floor under her paws began to rumble and shake as the truck pulled away.

A sudden, sharp change in direction knocked her off her feet. She got up again, bracing herself against one of the pallets this time. She cursed herself for being so stupid. How could she have risked this? Where was this truck going?

Taking a breath, she refocused. It probably wasn't going too far. She carefully made her way to the back of the truck and lay down, preserving her energy. As soon as that door opened again, she would jump out and get away. She braced herself, her muscles tight with fear, and tried to stay alert.

The truck drove along for hours. The steady rumble and the swaying motion made her eyelids feel so heavy. After a while, remembering the package of bread beside her, she tore it open and ate a huge meal. She would need energy when they finally stopped. Her stomach twisted thinking of how much ground the truck was covering. She laid her head down with a sigh, feeling her full belly. She fought the urge to sleep.

A high metallic squeal woke her up. How long had she been asleep? Her tongue was stuck against the roof of her mouth, and she tried to remember the last time she had drunk any water. Then her stomach clenched. Scruff. He didn't know where she was or what had happened to her. How far away was she now? How was she going to get back to him?

FIVE
GONE

Scruff

The pads of Scruff's paws were swollen from walking all night. He had heard Pica leaving when darkness fell, and as soon as he was certain she'd gone, he went off in the opposite direction. His frustration and anger pushed him to go farther than he normally would have, letting his feet pick the path and automatically changing directions if he smelled another coyote.

Thoughts of Pica swirled around his brain as he picked his way along the edge of a neighbourhood, past houses and cars dark and silent. She could be so stubborn. Here she was, injured and starving in the middle of winter, and she wouldn't eat a single bite of the food because he had stolen it in a way that was against their code. Couldn't she see that desperate times called for desperate measures?

The hours passed quickly as he walked lost in thought, and he was surprised when the sky began to lighten. He stopped, becoming aware of his throbbing paws, and realized that he was in an entirely unfamiliar area. He paused to take stock of his situation. He had unconsciously headed downhill, and now he could smell the salt of the ocean just a few blocks away. Train tracks followed the shape of the coastline, and there were lots of big roads, parking lots, and buildings. There were fewer houses here, and they weren't as big as the ones up the hill.

He knew instinctively that he wouldn't be able to get back to Pica before it was full daylight, and besides, being in a new environment, it would be dangerous to try. Besides, his sore muscles and paws were pleading with him to lie down. He began to travel more slowly, looking for a good place to curl up for the day. By the side of a big parking lot, he smelled water, and his nose led him to a deep ravine. Garbage was scattered down the embankments, but there was little sign of human activity, and he realized suddenly how thirsty he was. It was worth further investigation.

Scruff circled the area slowly before entering it, as he always did. He sniffed each bush along the top of the ravine, looking for any scent markers that would warn him that the area was taken by another coyote. At the third bush, he stopped in his tracks, his skin tingling. He raised his head, looking around nervously, then lowered his head to sniff again. It couldn't be. The fresh scent radiating off of the scrubby oak bush was unmistakably Jagger's. The last time he had seen Jagger was at the golf course where Pica grew up, which was over the bridge and through a dangerous park, a few days' travel away. Why would Jagger have travelled here to the Wild Lands, too?

He didn't wait to find out. Whirling around, he galloped away from the ravine, putting a good distance between himself and that smell. As the sky turned from peach to pink to light grey, he kept up a good pace, stopping only when it was full daylight. He chose a large clump of bushes that was practically on the street, but it was a quiet street, and he thought he'd be able to pass the day here undisturbed.

Jagger's smell had unlocked a flood of memories. He had been a young pup, unable to care for himself, when his parents and all his siblings died. Jagger had rescued him, keeping him safe and fed, though he'd never provided much in the way of love. Scruff owed his life to the older coyote who, he later found out, was actually his brother from a previous litter. But his feelings were complicated by Jagger's scheming. When humans built houses over their forest home, Jagger had decided to take over Pica's family's territory right next door. Scruff's stomach turned as he remembered the part he'd played, luring Pica's father away from the rest of the family, not knowing at the time what Jagger's plan was. Pica's family had lost the golf course, and their father, because of him. He had been young and naive then. But not now. He renewed his resolve to get back to Pica and patch things up. He'd have to tell her about Jagger, of course, but they could always go somewhere else, somewhere far away, once again putting Jagger out of their lives.

As soon as the light faded, Scruff was on his feet again. His belly felt hollow, and his muscles were stiff from travelling so far, then spending the day curled in a tense ball. Heading back uphill felt good, though. He was ready to put some distance between him and Jagger and to talk to Pica. His body softened a little bit, thinking about her. His anger was gone, replaced with an urgent need to patch things up. He had been stupid to go in that truck. He'd return with a mouse to show her that he was ready to hunt like a coyote again.

It was a long haul back to the power lines, but Scruff kept up a steady pace, and at the end of the night, he was finally entering the familiar neighbourhood. Time to find a mouse now. He pricked his ears forward, sniffing the air carefully, and entered an alley behind a row of hulking, dark houses. As he passed a garbage can, he heard a distinctive rustle. Pausing with one paw in the air, he homed in on the sound. With two quick steps, he leapt high into the air, stretching his paws out toward the spot and snatching the mouse in his jaws, giving it a firm shake. He gave a muffled yip. A clean shot.

He covered the last few blocks quickly, his heart starting to beat faster as he reached the power lines. The mouse tasted delicious in his mouth. He couldn't wait to share it with Pica. But when he got to their spot under the power lines, he frowned, puzzled. There was no sign of her. Dropping the prey, he quickly circled the area. There was no fresh sign of her at all — she hadn't returned the previous day. Was she still mad at him?

Sighing, he lay down to wait. The smell of the mouse right next to his nose made his stomach hurt. It was really hard not to want to eat it right away. But he thought about how happy Pica would be when she got back, tired and hungry, and he curled up tightly around his prize.

He fell deeply asleep at some point, until bright light awoke him. It had been so long since he'd seen bright sunshine that he instinctively rolled over, exposing his fur to the warming sun. He yawned, lifting his head to look around, but felt a jolt in his body when he discovered there was still no Pica. Hurt, he ate the mouse, crunching it noisily and half hoping that she would wander in at that exact moment. Then she'd be sorry she was so late.

Now that it was daytime, he was stuck there. The hours passed slowly, and each small sound made him perk up his ears, hoping she was back. When darkness fell again, his mood became dark, too. He started to consider the possibility that Pica wasn't coming back. Was she so mad at him that she had decided never to return? Had she decided to return to her family?

The next few nights were a blur. He traced every inch of the surrounding area in every direction. He questioned every coyote he found. Some were rude, and some were kind, but none had seen a young, slim, grey coyote travelling on her own. He smelled her everywhere, but all the scent paths were old. She had simply disappeared, and he had no idea how to find her, or if she even wanted to be found.

PART TWO
PICA

PART TWO

PICA

SIX

WOLF

Pica lay on the cold metal floor of the truck for many hours, waiting for something to change. Each passing moment tore deep into her as she felt her distance from Scruff increasing. At long last, the truck's movements began to change. It slowed down and turned several corners. Pica jumped to her feet in anticipation.

Finally, the truck groaned to a complete stop, and the engine shut off. Pica could hear humans talking and footsteps approaching the big sliding door. Her body tensed as she prepared for whatever came next. With a screech of metal, the door opened, and bright light blinded her. She squinted, trying to see an escape. One of the humans let out a loud shout when he spotted her. She couldn't wait any longer. Even though her eyes hadn't adjusted yet, she leapt out of the back of the truck, falling hard onto the ground.

Before she could get away, something hard and heavy hit her already tender side. She struggled to regain her breath and looked up, finally able to see again. The dark shape of a man hulked over her. He had a long stick in his hands. With two quick bounds, Pica was up and out of reach.

Ducking her head, she raced toward some trees. She felt a stinging sensation on her back — the human was throwing rocks at her. She tripped, rolling painfully across hard ground. Sensing a car coming on her left, she got up again and ran. Once she reached the small stand of trees, she dove into the bushes.

She flipped around to peer out and saw more humans gathered now, still yelling. They started walking toward her across the large parking lot. They knew where she was. She wasn't safe here. She looked around frantically. Where could she go? Behind her was the road. There were a few cars travelling along it, but still it seemed safer than the parking lot. She sprinted out of the far side of the bushes and into the ditch along the side of the road. As she passed a few more buildings, she found herself in an open area with big fields on either side of the road. On the far side of one of the fields, she saw what looked like a forest.

Leaving the cover of the ditch, she ran across the field. Breathing harder and harder, she dug her claws into the soft grass, willing her body to go faster. She felt sharp pains where the big cat had injured her, but she couldn't stop. Not now. It felt as if she were moving in slow motion.

Finally, she entered the forest. It was only a small stand of trees, but there were no humans around. Her sides heaving in and out, she tried to hear over the sound of her own gasping breath. There was nothing but the wind. She peeked out at the field. No one was pursuing her. As her breath calmed, she began to notice other senses. Her back and sides burned, and she could feel fresh blood oozing out of her cuts. Her legs shook. Her nose was assaulted by new scents of animals she had never encountered before. It all felt completely foreign. Without a doubt, she was very far from home.

She stayed there in the stand of trees for a long time, observing more and more as she got used to the new environment. First of all, the cold here was different. In the Wild Lands and in the city, the air was damp. Here, it was dry, with a biting wind whipping across the fields. A dusting of snow lay on the ground. The sun shone, but it gave off little heat. Around her, the land opened up to the sky in a way she had never seen before. Where she came from, there were trees, buildings, and hillsides rising up all around. She'd felt safe there, nestled in between familiar landmarks. Here, the horizon was flat, the cold blue sky meeting the edge of the world many miles away. She could see some roads and buildings in the direction she had fled from, and she could hear a large highway in the distance, but besides that, there was nothing.

The late afternoon sun was low in the sky now. She couldn't let her mind spin out anymore. Her plan was obvious. Find food and water. Start heading back to Scruff.

Hopefully, it wouldn't take too long to get back to the city. She'd wait for darkness to fall, then head out. However, she realized with a sinking feeling that she wasn't quite sure which direction she'd come from in the truck.

When darkness finally fell, she cautiously emerged from the stand of trees and crossed back through the field toward the road. Now that she didn't have to run, she noticed large animals standing in the field, grouped together. One bellowed as it saw her, then they all raised their heads and stared at her. They were massive, and she had never seen anything like them in the city or in the Wild Lands, but something told her they weren't dangerous. All the same, she gave them a wide berth.

She reached the road and followed it toward the distant sounds of a bigger road. The truck had travelled so far that she knew she'd have to follow the biggest road she could find. She didn't have to walk in the ditch now; in the dark, no cars were using the road. She trotted along the centre line with a view of fields and low buildings in every direction. All the empty space made her uncomfortable. She felt exposed and, in the velvety blackness of the night, completely alone.

It wasn't long until she encountered more buildings and eventually came to a small town at a junction between the road she was travelling and a bigger road. Even now, the cold wind was whipping around the buildings, sending trash flying in the air and ruffling her fur. She paused in the bushes in front of the big road. It was wide, but not busy. An occasional truck roared past, but for the most part, it felt as dead as everything else here.

Her pulse raced as she looked around. She had no idea which way she had come from in the truck. She scanned one direction, then the other, but they looked the same to her, and there were no familiar smells to guide her. Taking a deep breath, she forced herself to focus. Examining the first direction again, she noticed that the road ran between two low hills, disappearing into the distance as it dipped downhill, out of sight. In the other direction, the road rose slowly toward a few bumps on the horizon. She squinted — were they trees? She took a deep breath, sniffing the air carefully for any clues. Some kind of feeling was telling her to go toward the little bumps, but she didn't know what they were. Should she trust it?

The only thing she did know was that she couldn't stay here. She'd have to trust her instinct. With one last, long glance in the other direction, she turned up the road toward the small bumps and began a steady lope toward what she hoped was home.

At first, she felt invigorated. Cold air rushed into her lungs, and the strange night sounds seemed sharper. She stayed alert, keeping the road to her left and staying in the longer grasses in case she came upon something dangerous. None of the passing cars and trucks slowed down as they whooshed past, sweeping their bright headlights over her. She felt like she was making quick progress. After a few hours, though, her stomach began to grumble, and her back and sides were sore, especially when she breathed in.

After a few more hours, her leg muscles began to shake, so she took a break. Lowering her belly to the frozen earth, she groaned. What was worse, trotting along, exhausted, or shivering here on the ground? Ignoring her discomfort, she laid her head on her paws and closed her eyes, telling herself she'd just take a short rest before setting off again. She did need food, but that, too, would have to wait. She let her heavy eyelids fall closed with relief.

A chilling howl woke her. It was unmistakable — the sound of a coyote in grave danger. Pica jumped to her feet before she was fully awake and ducked deeper into the long grasses, crouching low. Frantic yips came from a different direction. Suddenly, she saw a shadow moving through the darkness past her. It was a coyote, and he was running flat out. He must be running away from something. Casting a nervous glance back into the darkness, she leapt up and began to follow him. She, too, had to get far away from whatever was chasing him. When the coyote rounded a clump of large bushes, though, she lost him. She peered nervously back into the darkness again and swivelled her ears. Nothing. She took a few breaths, the cold air cutting into her lungs. She felt alone and small in this expansive, dark world.

She stealthily crept around the bushes and peeked out. The road was a dark shadow. A huge coyote was crouched over a large lump on the road. Pica noticed another shape to her right and recognized the coyote she had been following. No one moved.

Pica felt the hair on her neck rise. The large coyote didn't smell right ... then she understood. This animal wasn't actually a coyote at all. Its chest rippled with muscles, and its massive head rose up from a thick neck. Rooted to the spot, Pica tried to puzzle out what it was. Her wonder turned to icy fear as the creature's head swung around, and narrowed, glittering eyes stared straight at her.

SEVEN
STANDOFF

For a moment, the large, golden eyes drew Pica in. Her legs felt too heavy to move. She looked downward and took a submissive posture, not knowing what else to do.

Then, the coyote barked, "Leave my brother alone, wolf!" making Pica jump with surprise. With the word *wolf*, it all came together. She remembered her parents telling stories to her and her siblings in the long, hot afternoons at the golf course, back when they were young. Stories of massive creatures, not from the city, who were a bit like coyotes, but much larger and stronger, and much more dangerous. She glanced up at the wolf and at the lump lying below it, then gasped. Was that the coyote's brother? She wasn't sure how she'd found herself in the middle of this situation, but she dreaded how it would end.

"I'll leave your brother alone when you leave my food alone," the wolf growled back, her voice a deep, resonating growl. Her paw was firmly planted on the lump in front of her. Pica became dimly aware of the smell of fresh deer and the emptiness of her stomach.

At that moment, she felt a rumble in her paws, and seconds later came the sound of a truck driving quickly toward them. Abandoning the standoff, Pica leapt off the road and ducked low into the grass. The other coyote and the wolf did the same. Even the shape on the ground crawled awkwardly out of the way.

The truck passed with a roar, slowing down slightly when its headlights picked up the carcass of a deer at the side of the road, but continued along. The others immediately resumed their standoff: the coyote on one side of the carcass, the wolf on the other. Pica cautiously took a few steps backward, hoping to leave the scene without anyone noticing.

The second coyote — the one who had been underneath the wolf — rose slowly, joining his brother, and spoke now. He was young, about her age, but more muscled. "I was here first. The deer isn't yours. It's ours." He motioned with his head toward the other coyote and Pica. Pica's eyes widened. She had become part of the negotiation.

The wolf stared them down in turn, not moving an inch. "My pack is on its way. Leave now or we'll show no mercy."

"I don't hear them." Pica was surprised at the almost cocky tone of the second coyote. His confidence outstripped his size. "You can move along now, and just let us know when they arrive."

The wolf's eyes narrowed to slits. The first coyote took a step forward so he was standing shoulder-to-shoulder with his brother. Then the wolf directed her stare at Pica, lifting her upper lip in a snarl that exposed long white teeth.

"Who is this you've brought to help strengthen your sad little pack? Is she even a coyote? She's so small and skinny. More like a mouse," she scoffed.

Pica felt the fur rise along her back and neck and changed her posture to an aggressive one. Glaring back at the wolf, she recalled Jagger staring her down with the same contempt, confident in his physical size and his power over her. Back then, he'd known that all he had to do was intimidate her, and she would give up and run away. Now, she was miles and miles away from home, yet it was happening all over again.

Without thinking of the consequences, she took three slow steps forward, straight toward the wolf. Staring into those mesmerizing yellow eyes, she responded with the lowest growl she could manage. "You have absolutely no idea who I am or what I can do. Try me."

The wolf frowned, looking her up and down. Pica took another step, her tail sticking straight up behind her. She was close enough to see the wolf's sides moving in and out as she breathed. A moment of complete stillness passed.

Then, sweeping her eyes over all three of the young coyotes, the wolf exhaled loudly and turned away. She glided a few feet down the road before turning back, her eyes settling on Pica. "I won't forget about you, Mouse. You won't always be with these clowns, and I won't always be alone. Watch your back."

Pica shivered but maintained her posture and continued to watch the wolf. She stayed frozen like that until the wolf had faded into the night.

"Hey, thanks! You were amazing!" yipped the second coyote, dancing around Pica. He seemed completely unhurt now. Up close, the moonlight glinted off his reddish fur.

"Yeah, who are you, anyway?" chimed in the other one.

"Never seen you around before."

"Nope, me either."

"She sure told that wolf."

"She sure did."

They talked over top of each other, bouncing around her happily. They were cut off by an approaching truck, but as soon as it passed, they resumed their chatter. Pica looked quickly from one to the other as they talked, waiting for a brief pause to jump in, but it never came.

"Man, if you hadn't arrived, I don't know."

"Wolves, man."

"I know, right? They're such bullies."

"But then you came and —"

"We were definitely going to have to leave."

They turned to each other, still talking.

"I got here first, that's why I called you."

"I know! I came."

"But you were so slow!"

"I came as fast as I could."

"Why were you so far away?"

"Rabbit."

"Oh."

"But even with you —"

"I know — we needed three."

"And then she arrived."

"Right. Wait, who are you again?"

With that, they finally paused, both pairs of eyes staring at her. Pica shook her head.

"I —"

"You're definitely not from around here."

"Dude, let her finish!" shushed the red one. "Don't mind my brother. He likes to talk."

Pica cocked her head to the side slightly and stifled a smile. She took a deep breath. "I'm Pica. Nice to meet you."

"Rip," nodded the red one.

"Rooney," added the brown one. "We're brothers."

Pica waited a second to make sure he was done, then added, "I'm just passing through, actually. I'm following this highway back to the city. I just happened to be near here. Glad I could help."

Rooney cocked his head. "What's the city?"

Rip responded. "You know, the big place with all the humans. Mom's talked about it before."

Rooney nodded. "Right. But how did you get all the way here?"

Pica hesitated. But just as she opened her mouth, her stomach growled loudly, interrupting her. The smell of the meat was still in the air.

Rip looked sympathetic. "Sorry, we tend to talk a lot. You must be hungry. Let's dig in while we can. Never know who'll get here first — our pack or hers. Strength in numbers, out here. If the wolves get here first, we'll have to get away fast. I don't think our pack is too far, though, and I'm sure they heard us."

Pica followed the brothers to the deer carcass, her legs wobbly after all of the excitement. She helped them drag it off the road so they could eat in peace. She kept glancing around, wondering if they could be sure that the wolf wasn't coming back. Now that it was all over, all of her bravado had left her. She needed to get some food and get out of here.

She watched as Rip and Rooney used their sharp teeth and claws to rip past the thick outer hide to the meat inside. They moved over to make room for her, and she cautiously took a few bites. It was delicious, warm and chewy. She could feel her stomach filling with each bite. Suddenly, her fur stood up again, and her stomach clenched. She heard howls and footsteps in the distance, heading straight for them. She jumped back.

"Chill, Pica." Rooney lifted his head to nod at her. "No worries. That's our mom, Leila, and the pack."

"Reinforcements!" Rip laughed, his mouth full. They both tore back into the meal. Pica waited as six or seven shadows came into view. She admired how they trotted smoothly, moving as one.

"Rip! Rooney! Are you okay?" A tall, thin female approached and sniffed them carefully, working her nose all the way down their bodies. "Rip — what's that?"

"Aw, Mom, was nothing. Just a wolf again. It's a scratch, is all."

The older coyote inhaled sharply. "What were you doing, confronting a wolf without us?"

"I got here first, and she came up on me so fast, I didn't even sense her."

"We've talked about this. Find the kill, call us, and wait for us."

Rip hung his head. "Yes, Mom." He looked up at her with a grin. "But Rooney came to help really quickly, and then Pica came, too. She was amazing — the wolf said she was scrawny and small like a mouse, but then she puffed up so big and said, 'Don't call me a mouse!' and scared that wolf right away!"

Pica felt hot as Rip retold the story. She suddenly felt eight pairs of coyote eyes staring at her. Leila approached her, sniffing her carefully. Pica stayed completely still, standing deferentially, barely breathing. Leila was clearly the alpha of the group.

"Where are you from?"

Rooney jumped in with excitement. "She's from the city."

Leila frowned. "The city? Then why are you here?"

Pica opened her mouth, then closed it. She tried again. "It's … a long story," she hedged.

Leila gave a quick nod. "Okay. Well, for now, we eat. You can tell me more later." She gave a sign to the pack, and the coyotes attacked the meal with vigour, eight sets of teeth and claws tearing chunks off. Rip glanced over at her with a small smile. "Get in there, Pica, or there'll be nothing left. You've earned it!"

With that, Pica dove in, too, feeling warm bodies on either side of her. She ate and ate, her belly expanding around the meat. She hadn't eaten this well since she'd lived on the golf course with her family. She gobbled up much more meat than she typically ate in a day, knowing that it might be days before her next meal, and that every bite would give her strength to return to Scruff.

She had just licked her lips after finishing her last bite when she heard a long howl, followed by another, then another. The wolf was back, and she wasn't alone this time.

EIGHT
ICE MOUNTAINS

Pica's fur stood on end. As soon as one wolf howl ended, the song was taken up by others, their voices weaving in and out until there was a solid wall of sound. All of the coyotes sprang to their feet around her, looking attentively to Leila for a signal. She nodded and led them off at a gallop in the opposite direction to the howls.

"You'd better come with us," Rip called to Pica. "They'll kill you if they find you here alone."

Pica hesitated. The coyotes were not headed in the direction that she wanted to go. Following them would mean losing valuable time backtracking. On the other hand, she wasn't completely certain that she was going the right way, and being completely alone, she was very vulnerable. As another howl sent shivers down her back, her body made the decision for her, turning to race after the pack.

She settled into an awkward gallop, her stomach a heavy rock swinging from side to side and pulling down the skin around her ribs. After a short sprint, the pack slowed down. The other coyotes were groaning with the weight of their meal, too. Rip dropped back to trot beside her. His ears swivelled toward her, and Pica noticed there was a chunk missing from one of them. The look in his eyes was curious. "So how have you managed to survive out here alone?"

Pica looked away, searching for answers in the dark, flat landscape around her. "Well …" She paused, buying time while her thoughts raced. "I haven't been out here for that long, actually. Like I said, I'm from the city." She glanced over to gauge Rip's reaction. His brow furrowed.

"Wait, so you crossed the ice mountains all by yourself? Made it through wolf territory? And now you're just turning around?"

What were the ice mountains? Her stomach dropped. She would have to find out more about that before she left these coyotes. If she stayed with them for a few hours, she might be able to get the information she needed without giving away too much. She looked away again and tried to make her voice sound casual. "Uh, yep, I crossed the mountains." Technically it was true. She had made it through the mountains on her own, in the truck.

"Uh, okay. I guess you were kind of fierce when we were up against that wolf. Pretty good for a small — well, I'm not calling you small, just young, you know. Like me.

Not full grown yet." He stumbled over his words, trying not to insult her.

She hid her smile. As long as he was distracted, he might drop the line of questioning.

"Rip!" Leila's voice broke into their conversation as she called him up to trot with her at the front of the pack.

"Sorry, gotta go. I've got more questions, though!"

"No worries. Later is fine."

He sped up his trot to catch up with Leila. Pica could hear his voice up at the front.

"Yes, Mom?"

"What were you thinking back there, getting in the way of a wolf? You know better than that."

Rip begin an apology, and Pica tuned out of the conversation. It reminded her of so many she had had with her parents whenever she had done something foolish. A flood of memories washed over her, bathing her in the sounds and smells of her past. She had always been the one in her family to push the boundaries, and here, running away from a wolf with strange coyotes in a strange new land, she felt like the situation was again her fault. She resolved to make good decisions going forward — starting with getting more information about how to get home.

A short while later, they arrived at a spot with short, gnarly trees growing along a slow-moving creek. The sun was up now, casting light and weak warmth on Pica's fur. She could tell from the smell that this was the pack's home territory. The coyotes all began to relax, drinking deeply from a small pool at a bend in the creek and then scattering to find soft areas to lie down. Some groomed each other, others curled up to digest their food. Pica drank deeply and then sat down to take stock of her injuries, checking to see how her wounds were healing after such a wild day and night. Had it only been that long? It seemed like a lifetime ago that she was curled up with Scruff under the power lines.

Leila walked over to her. Pica felt herself stiffening. She flattened her ears and looked up to see eyes of intense, molten gold. She couldn't look away.

"So, you're from the city."

Pica nodded. "Yes."

"I know of it, but I've never been there. I'm curious to know how you got here."

"Well, actually I'm just passing through on my way back." Pica gave the same answer she had given Rip, but it didn't land well. Leila shook her head.

"That doesn't explain how you got here."

"It's kind of a weird story."

Leila just waited, and the silence got awkward. Pica cast about for any excuse, not knowing how much she could trust these new coyotes, but Leila's piercing eyes made her feel so uncomfortable that she found herself telling her story. Leila had a strength and determination that Pica hadn't encountered since she'd left her own mother, Gree. As she talked, Pica noticed other coyotes drawing closer to listen. By the end, they were all staring at her. Leila had listened intently all the way through, not showing surprise or judgment. Now she turned to others, addressing them in a stern tone.

"That is why we don't trust humans. They are the source of many unexpected problems." Her tone softened as she turned back to Pica. "You helped Rip and Rooney, and our pack is grateful to you for that. You are welcome to stay with us for now. You will be safe here."

Pica nodded. "Thank you. I'm very … appreciative of the offer." She searched for the right words, trying not to offend. "But … I really need to get back to my family. I have to get back to the Wild Lands as quickly as I can. Can you tell me how to get there?"

Leila looked down at her, squinting. "Well, I don't know these Wild Lands you speak of. But I do know of the city, and I can direct you there. You must know, however, that the journey will be a very dangerous one. It's a long, long way, and the mountains are full of ice at this time of the year. I don't think it's a good idea to try crossing them in winter. Especially since you are still healing from whatever attacked you."

Pica's breath came faster and faster. She saw the sense in what Leila was saying, but waiting until summer — that was so far away! And by then, Scruff might have moved on, and she might not be able to find him. He might even find someone else to start a new pack with. She inhaled deeply and slowly, trying to calm her thoughts. "I hear what you say, but I have to try. I don't have time to wait until summer."

Leila regarded her, clearly weighing things in her mind. "All right. Lie down with me here. I'll tell you everything I know. You should rest for a few hours and leave at midday. The wolves are most active at dusk and at dawn, and as a small one, you're going to have to do everything you can to avoid them."

"Okay." Pica shivered. She lay down and listened intently for the next hour as Leila told her all the stories she had heard and everything she knew about wolf activity in the area. Then Leila examined Pica's cuts and pronounced them to be healing well. Finally, she stood and nodded, dismissing Pica and padding over to another coyote to talk softly with him.

Pica stood awkwardly and looked for a place to lie down by herself, not wanting to accidentally take another coyote's spot.

"You can lie down over here," Rip called out helpfully.

Pica walked over and found a patch of long, soft grass beside him. She flopped down, exhausted. Rip closed his eyes and began breathing slowly and evenly. With the musical sound of the creek and Rip's soft breathing, Pica relaxed enough to sink into a deep sleep.

NINE
TRAP

Pica dozed off and on, watching the pack around her interact and waiting for the sun to get high enough in the sky for her to leave. No one spoke to her, but they didn't seem worried about her being there. Leila padded around, checking in with everyone, although it was clear that she was closest to a large male coyote, Bruno. They acted differently from her parents, though, and she could tell from Bruno's smell that he was related to Leila. He was likely her pup from a few years ago. He was large and muscled and had an air of confidence, directing the others when Leila wasn't around. She wondered where Leila's mate was and what had happened to him.

The others all seemed to be related, too. Other than Rip and Rooney, there were two females about the same size, and from the way they all interacted, she guessed the four of them were siblings from the same year's litter. Finally, there was another female who was older than them, but not as old as Leila. Probably another one of her pups from a year or two ago. Pica had never seen such a big pack before, and she wondered if this was common out here. She guessed having a big pack was useful when there were wolves around, and there was certainly more space out here than there was in the city.

When the sun was finally at its highest point, she rose and stretched. Rip, who had been munching on some grass a little ways away, came over to give her a gentle sniff. "Good luck," he said, frowning. "I really don't know that it's a good idea, though, heading out there on your own."

Pica laughed, acknowledging the truth of the statement. "What choice do I have?"

"Well ..." Rip looked at her, considering. "If you just waited until the warm season, you'd be bigger, and the mountains would be a lot easier to cross."

Pica gave a half-smile, but she couldn't wait one more minute. "I have to go." Her voice came out more confident than she actually felt. Her stomach was fluttering nervously.

Leila came over with Bruno. They each touched noses with her gently. "Keep alert and avoid the wolves," Leila instructed. She gestured up the highway. "Follow that road. Soon you'll see the mountains. Follow the road up and over, and if you're lucky, you'll be back in the city within a few days. Be as quick as possible. Every day you spend alone out here is dangerous."

"Thanks, Leila. I really appreciate it." With a firm nod, Pica set off, aware that every coyote in the pack was watching her go. She kept her head up, adopting a steady pace that she hoped she'd be able to keep up. She felt strong after the huge meal she'd had the previous night, although her muscles protested the familiar trotting motion.

Returning to the highway, she retraced her steps back to where the deer was. The road was a lot busier during the day, a constant stream of cars and trucks passing in either direction. She veered away, out of sight of the humans driving on the road, but stayed within earshot. She didn't want to go anywhere near that deer carcass, either, even though the wolves had probably moved on by now. The ground fell away under her as she passed through field after field. Each time she rose to the top of a gentle hill, she tensed, ready to see the ice mountains. But each time, all that met her gaze were more hills rolling off into the distance.

For a while, she followed a creek that paralleled the road. As she passed one bush, there was an explosion, and a bird surged out from underneath it, clearly panicked. Pica leapt toward it and snapped her jaws, surprising herself when she felt the warm body in her mouth. She paused to eat, then found three eggs in the nest and ate those, too. She drank deeply from the creek, celebrating her success. Energy flooded into her, and she began to believe that she might actually make it. If she hurried, Scruff would still be waiting for her.

As dusk fell, she started looking for a place to hide out. Leila's warning about wolves hunting at dusk rang in her head. She glanced over her shoulder constantly, thinking she had heard something. If she stopped now for a rest, she could continue in the middle of the night, when the wolves would hopefully have gone to sleep.

She descended to the bottom of a valley and circled closer and closer to a house. She had so far avoided humans, but as scared as she was of them, she was more scared of wolves. According to Leila, if she could take shelter near a house, wolves were less likely to be nearby. She found a creek behind a large red barn. The smells and sounds of humans and animals drifted faintly on the chilly evening air. Taking a few more moments to sniff around and make sure there were no other animals around, she chose a big bush and crept underneath, digging her claws into the frozen, crusty ground to expose the warmer layer of earth underneath. She curled up tight, tucking her nose under her tail. Her eyes stayed open — heavy, but alert.

Some time later, something jolted her from sleep. In a flash, she was on her feet outside the bush, heart racing. What was it? She swivelled her ears and tested the air with each nostril. Then she heard it again. A wolf howl, and not far from here. She hesitated, wondering if she was safe, but the wolves sounded too close. She took off in the opposite direction, running stiffly as her cold muscles took time to warm up. It wouldn't be long until they smelled her.

She gave the big human building a wide berth and set off into open fields. She was heading away from the road, but she couldn't worry about that now. An old wooden fence marked a boundary on a steep hillside. She slipped under it easily and continued on to a large meadow. With no trees or bushes around to give cover, she was acutely aware of how exposed she was. At the far side of the meadow, a stand of trees loomed tall in the darkness, so she increased her pace, aiming for them.

Arriving at the edge of the trees, she felt a sharp pain in her side and stopped to catch her breath, her panting breath making vapour trails in the cold air. A blood-chilling sound broke the stillness. One howl became many. The wolf pack had found each other, and they were hunting something.

Pica's feet were rooted to the ground. Her whole body was screaming at her not to leave the cover of the trees, but if the wolves were hunting her, they would easily follow her scent trail and find her here. She craned her neck to look down the hill, waiting for a sign in the darkness. A moment later, she heard another howl. It was much closer this time. They were coming for her.

Abandoning the trees, she sprinted through another meadow, heading away from the howling. As she crested a small hill, she risked a glance behind her. Four grey shapes were silhouetted in the distance, yipping. They were headed straight for her.

Without a parting glance, she ran, lengthening her stride and pushing herself to new limits. Meadows blurred past as the ground rolled under her. She streaked past a dark farmhouse, running too close by in her panic. Inside, a dog barked loudly, causing her to veer away and trip over her feet. She rolled twice, wincing in pain, and jumped up again. The wolves were gaining on her. She could hear their footsteps now. Desperate, she looked around for an escape, but the land was flat and open, with nowhere to hide.

At the next hill, she began to slow down. Her body was numb, and she was finding it harder and harder to breathe. Her paw hit a divot in the ground, and she stumbled again, yelping in pain as one of her old wounds hit a sharp rock. The next howl was deafeningly close. By the time she regained her feet, she knew she was beaten, and she turned to meet her fate.

The huge female wolf from the previous night stood before her, flanked by three other wolves all smaller than her, but still much larger than Pica. Their large bodies surrounded her, a wall of muscle and fur.

"Mouse," the lead wolf growled, "we meet again." Chills rolled through Pica's body. The other wolves huffed in excitement, hunger and darkness in their eyes. One of the smaller wolves was trembling slightly and took a step toward her. "Back!" snapped the lead wolf. Her tone was so commanding that Pica almost jumped back, too.

The smaller wolf cowered. "Sorry, Skye. It's just that I'm hungry and —"

" Enough!" Skye barked. "We're all hungry. It's been a long winter. But this is my coyote." She turned her attention back to Pica. "You ate our food, Mouse. You're trespassing on our land. It seems you don't respect us at all."

Pica scanned the meadow, desperately wishing to see Leila, Bruno, or any of the other coyotes, but only a cold wind swept over the tall grasses. No one was coming to save her. There was no way out.

Then, in the distance, a large truck started its engine. All four wolves turned toward the sound, ears twitching. Pica glimpsed a gap in the circle they'd formed around her and dashed through, fleeing straight toward the noise. As scary as humans could be, it was nothing compared to the jaws of four hungry wolves. Her small head start might just get her there before they caught up.

Yelps of surprise and anger gave way to thundering paws in pursuit. Pica's claws dug into the dirt as she raced as fast as she could, but in mere seconds, she felt the first stinging graze of teeth on her flank. They were too strong and fast.

She heard a warning bark from Skye and felt the other wolves drop away. She glanced back to see what had happened. The wolves had all stopped and were watching her run away. She frowned, slowing down herself to think. What would stop a pack of wolves in their tracks? She turned her attention to the land around her, smelling and listening for some other danger. Hopping over a small creek, she slowed to a walk, placing her paws carefully. She couldn't sense anything besides the cold wind and the distant hum of the truck engine.

But still … there was something bad about this place. She couldn't quite place the threat. Going back was not an option, but she wasn't sure about continuing onward, either. As she walked, her whole body felt electric, waiting for something to happen. When she glanced back a moment later, the wolves were gone; they'd melted into the night as quickly as they had come. She felt a pang of longing for the houses and cars of the city. At least there, she knew what the dangers were. Here, there were dark, mysterious menaces.

The gentle gurgling of a creek nearby calmed her breathing a little. She would get a drink of water and then lie down for a bit to wait for the wolves to get farther away. Then she'd retrace her steps back to the road. She needed to get out of wolf territory as fast as she could.

Her steps were tentative as she turned toward the creek. She paused. Something was wrong. She was sure of it. A long moment passed, then was broken by an owl hooting in the darkness. She shook her head. Maybe she was going crazy. She took one more step, and suddenly the ground gave way beneath her — there was a loud snapping sound. A lightning-hot pain shot up her left leg and seared through her whole body, coming in waves that took her breath away. She tried to jump up, but she couldn't get away. Something was wrapped around her front paw. She bit at it, but her teeth just scraped against cold metal. She pulled her paw back as hard as she could, bracing with her other three legs. Pain shot through her leg, but the metal did not give way. She was stuck.

TEN
STRUGGLE

Pica was barely aware of the morning's arrival. She pulled and twisted her trapped paw, bracing with her good front paw and feeling the steel jaws bite deeper and deeper into her skin. She tried gnawing at the trap, but the vibration of the metal against her teeth hurt her jaws and gave her a headache. Nothing she did made any difference, but she couldn't stop trying. She howled her frustration, so blinded by pain that she didn't even care if the wolves heard.

With each hour that passed she grew weaker. She could gnaw and pull only for a short time before dizziness overwhelmed her, and then she would fall to the ground, gasping for breath. Meadows stretched out in every direction to the sky. There was not even a tree to keep her company. The wind blew cold, and she shivered uncontrollably.

Her mouth was swollen and dry. The creek, just a short distance away but completely unreachable, seemed to be laughing at her.

The sun went down, and again it was night. She curled up into a ball, her body shaking. Closing her eyes, she began to face the inevitable. She would die here, likely fairly soon. Her sadness pressed her down into the cold earth, and the world around her slipped away.

Something woke her in the middle of the night. A mouse squeaking by the creek. She instinctively jumped up to go after it, but the steel jaws jerked her back. The pain seemed to reinvigorate her, and she started pulling again. Again and again, she pulled. She felt the trap give way just a little bit and redoubled her efforts, but she couldn't get it to open any further. Again, her body weakened, more quickly this time. She sat back, and a long, mournful howl ripped from her chest. She cried for her future, which she would never know. She cried for Scruff, who would never know what had happened to her. She cried for the world, which would just go on without her. Finally, she was done. She lay back down, spent, and closed her eyes, submitting to the blackness.

She felt someone gently licking her face. It must be Scruff hovering over her in worry. She sighed and drifted off again. Then the licking became more insistent, and with it came a whining. It wasn't Scruff's whine, though. Her consciousness rose up from out of a deep, dark hole. Pain shot back through her body as she woke and cracked open an eye. She saw brown, tawny fur.

"Pica?"

She cracked open the other eye and found herself staring into Leila's horrified eyes. "Oh, you're back. Good. You need to get up right now. You can't stay here a minute longer. The humans are coming."

Pica groaned. Her body felt like it was made of heavy, oozing metal. What was Leila doing here? Was this a dream? Leila nipped her shoulder, hard. Pica yelped and felt adrenalin pumping through her. No, she was awake, and this was happening. She shook her head and looked around. It was morning. She'd been here for a night, a day, and another night. How had Leila found her?

Leila nipped her again, barking, "Get onto your feet and rip that leg out of there! You have to. It's your only chance of survival."

Pica numbly followed orders. She rose stiffly, shaking a bit, and began to pull, grunting as her leg sparked with pain. She thought she felt it slip out a bit more, but the trap held tight.

"I've tried. I can't get it out."

"You'll have to chew it off, then."

Pica looked at her with horror. "What?"

"You have to get free. It's morning. If you stay much longer, the humans will come and kill you." Leila's tone was rough and urgent.

Pica was confused. Humans? She opened her mouth to ask a question, then closed it again. It didn't matter. If she didn't get free, she'd die one way or another. She felt an electric surge through her body. She braced her good paw against a small rock and threw herself backward, away from the trap. The metal clanked loudly as it caught her leg again and again. She stopped for a second, her sides heaving with the effort.

"Good. I think it's helping." Leila inspected the trap. She used her teeth to gnaw away at something. Pica was so disoriented that she couldn't tell if Leila was gnawing the trap or her leg. "Okay, try it again."

Pica threw herself backward again, and once again, the trap held. This time though, her paw slipped out a little bit more. Leila bent her head again and chewed, occasionally lifting her head to scan the area anxiously. "Okay, now try —"

A large truck started up in the distance. Both coyotes froze and listened, ears and noses twitching. The sound grew louder. It was headed toward them.

"No time!" Leila cried. "The human is coming now. You have to do it. Go!"

Pica went cold and numb. With a strangled battle cry, she threw her whole body backward, again and again. Pain circled around her and through her until she couldn't see anymore. Then, suddenly, she was falling back, tumbling down toward the creek. She was no longer attached to the metal trap.

She lay on her back, panting, her body on fire. Leila appeared above her. "They're almost here. Follow me."

Pica heard footsteps crunching through the frosty ground and saw a figure in the distance. She locked eyes with Leila and, taking a deep breath, rolled onto her three good legs. They shook, threatening to give out under her, but the adrenalin pumping through her body helped propel her after Leila.

Following the depression made by the creek, Leila led the way down the hill, taking care to stay out of sight. Pica heard the humans talking, but it was a distant sound now. She concentrated on her footing, which was difficult with only three working legs. Her odd gait reminded her of a year ago, when Jagger had attacked her and injured her leg. She'd escaped back then, and she could do it again.

Leila looked back at her then with an encouraging expression. "We're lucky. No dogs yet. If you can keep going, I think we'll be okay."

They took a few short breaks when Pica stumbled, but otherwise kept their slow, steady pace until they had made it back to Leila's home creek. Pica was vaguely aware of the other coyotes staring at her as she stumbled into their camp. Then she smelled the familiar bush where she'd slept before and collapsed underneath it. Blackness immediately returned.

She woke up feeling hungry. She was surrounded by warmth and steady breathing, and she realized that Rip and Rooney were sleeping on either side of her. As soon as she began to stir, Rip's head snapped up. He turned to her with worry on his face.

"You didn't last long out there by yourself."

Rooney raised his head, too, and glared at his brother. "Rip, she's basically dead. You could at least start with 'hello' and 'how do you feel.'"

"But I know how she feels. She's exhausted and her paw hurts. It's a pointless question."

"It's not pointless, it's polite."

"Why are you always so bossy?"

"Both of you, quiet." Leila's head came into Pica's field of vision as she leaned over the three of them. "Leave Pica in peace. If you want to bicker, go do it on the other side of the creek. She's exhausted and doesn't need to be in the middle of your silly arguments."

Rip and Rooney both looked down, ashamed. "Sorry," they both mumbled, and then Rip added, "we're happy to see you again, anyway."

"That's enough. Scram," Leila woofed. "I need to talk to Pica."

Rip and Rooney jumped up, and as they wandered away, Rip give Rooney's butt a little nip. Rooney whipped his head around and kicked out his leg, and they were off, chasing each other. Pica grinned weakly in spite of her pain. Her smile disappeared when she turned to see Leila's serious expression.

"I'm glad you were able to get out of that leg trap. Not many are so lucky." Leila paused to take a deep breath. "I've seen it before. Arnou — he was my partner for seven seasons and the father of all the other coyotes here — he got caught and died that way two years ago. Not at that farm, but in a similar trap." She was silent for a moment before continuing. "You're lucky you were caught so close to that farm — it's on our hunting route. I heard you as I was passing. There were wolves nearby, did you know that?"

Pica gave a wan smile. "I didn't get very far before I ran straight into them. I was running away from them — that's how I ended up there."

Leila nodded. "The only things wolves are afraid of are humans and traps. That's probably why they didn't follow you. In a way, the trap saved you."

"I don't feel like I was saved."

"I know. Your injury is bad. But for now, you're safe with us. You're not family, but you saved Rip and Rooney, and as much as they are idiots, we love them. We'll give you a safe place to rest and try to recover. Our pack is strong, and we have plenty of food here. We can share some of the meat that we get with you."

Pica peered at her, a little suspicious. "That's very kind of you. Where I come from, it isn't common for another pack to help out an injured coyote."

Leila nodded again. "You're right. Maybe it's because of Arnou." She was quiet for a moment. "Hopefully, you will heal enough to try your journey again in the spring. I've seen similar injuries before, and it is possible to go on with only three legs. But for now, your job is to rest and eat. We'll worry about everything else later."

"Thank you, Leila. I can't think properly yet, but I really appreciate everything you've done to help me, and your offer to feed me. But what if I don't heal …?" Pica stopped. Her emotions made it difficult to continue talking.

"It's possible. But you must stay positive. I'll try to make sure Rip and Rooney don't exhaust you with their bickering."

Pica smiled again. "Thanks."

Leila licked her gently, then padded off to talk with some of the other coyotes. Pica dropped her head back down again, hungry and exhausted. Her smile disappeared. She couldn't believe that once again, a coyote pack had to support her. Her paw was hanging off her leg, completely wrecked. She'd never heard of a three-legged coyote before. She would be a serious burden on this pack for a long time. She made a quiet vow to herself that even if she wasn't healthy enough in the spring, she'd head out anyway. Dying on her own terms would be better than waiting for the pack to tire of her and kick her out.

As she drifted off, her mind turned to Scruff. What was he was doing right now? Was he thinking of her? Did he understand that she wasn't mad at him anymore, but she couldn't get back to him? She felt a deep loss, realizing that he might never know how hard she was willing to try to find him again. And worrying that by the time she found him, it might be too late.

PART THREE
SCRUFF

ELEVEN

WAITING

Scruff leapt through the air, landing and snapping his jaws cleanly around a large rat. His catch gave him little joy. It had been a week since Pica had disappeared, and he still hadn't found a single clue as to where she'd gone. He returned to the power lines each night, exhausted, hoping to find her waiting there. But as the days passed, he felt more and more sure that she was not coming back.

One night, he returned to the base of the bridge that led back to the city, hoping to catch her scent. If he could only be sure that she had passed this way, then he would know what had happened. There were many reasons she might have wanted to return to her family. For one, they could provide for her much better than he could. Still, he worried. Why hadn't she told him? Would she really have made the long journey back on her own? He worried about her every moment he was awake.

Cold days and cold nights blurred together. As time passed, his hope dwindled completely, and one day, Scruff didn't return to the power lines. It wasn't a conscious decision; he just lacked the energy needed to walk the last few miles back. He had been hunting for mice by the train tracks that ran along the ocean's edge, and he found a dirty, abandoned beach beside the tracks to spend the day, curling up under a bush.

His head lay heavy on his paws, and he stared into space. The cold waves scraped against the beach rocks. The smell of garbage and seaweed clogged his nose. His fur was wet, but he didn't try to dry himself. A long day stretched ahead of him. He closed his eyes, hoping for sleep. There was a large rock poking into his stomach, but he didn't change his position. He wondered what would happen if he never moved again. No one would care. No one would notice.

He passed in and out of sleep for most of the day. As the sun set low over the water, he decided not to go anywhere that night. His body felt heavy, and he couldn't think of a reason to get up.

Just then, a gravelly voice cut through his fog.

"Hey."

He lifted his head slowly and gazed listlessly at a tall, slim coyote just visible through the bush. Cautiously, he stuck his head out to get a better look. The coyote's coat was silvery grey, and long, thin legs led up to a narrow chest. She was young, like him, but more filled out — healthier.

Fully awake, he got up and stepped carefully out of the bushes, keeping a few feet of distance between them. Was she going to challenge him? Had he missed picking up on her scent markings? Her posture was very relaxed, though, and soon Scruff began to relax, too.

"Where did you come from?" Her voice was low and curious.

"Nowhere." He hadn't meant to sound so brusque.

"What do you mean? I've never seen you here before."

"I can leave if this is your spot," he replied wearily, beginning to walk away.

"Well, you sure are cheerful. You hungry or something?"

He just kept walking. Suddenly, a blur passed in front of him, and he was forced to stop in order to avoid running into her.

"What's your problem?" she said. "I'm just trying to talk to you!"

"I'm not really interested in talking."

"Why not?"

He stared at her. He hadn't met anyone so stubborn since ... a small shudder passed through him. He had been trying to avoid thinking about Pica, but it seemed she was in the margins of every thought.

"Why don't you just leave me alone?" His response came out harsher than he had intended. He stepped around the other coyote and kept walking, but he heard her footsteps fall in behind him. He crossed the tracks and approached the busy road that paralleled the coastline. Arriving at the edge, he peered out from between long, thick grasses. The evening sky was slate grey, and rain was falling hard. As cars passed, their tires splashed through puddles. Scruff didn't want any part of this world. All he wanted was to go back to the bush and curl up. Shut it all out.

He stood there for a few moments with the strange coyote who had followed him. She seemed to read his mind. "Want to head back to the beach for a bit?"

Wordlessly, he turned around and headed back, his new shadow following him. He knew he was being rude, but he really didn't want to make friends right now. With a sigh, he curled up next to a large rock. After a moment, the other coyote sat next to him. This time, she was silent, gazing at him with large grey eyes.

His fur prickled under the scrutiny. After a minute, he couldn't stand it anymore. "All right, I give up. What do you want?" he said, glaring at her.

"Oh, you talk! Great!" The coyote tilted her head to the side. "What's your name, anyway?"

"Scruff."

She looked him up and down. "Suits you. I'm Kaia."

"Hi."

"Are you from around here? I don't remember smelling you before. I hang out in this park, but it's not mine, if you know what I mean. It's not much to defend, right? Not really worth the effort. Anyway, I was born near here — just down the road. My family still lives there, but I'm not really like them. I took off on my own last fall, and things have been going great …"

Once she got going, she didn't stop. Scruff had never met anyone who could talk so much. In under an hour, he found out all about her puppyhood growing up in a family of seven, about her parents' trouble finding enough food to feed all the pups, and about Kaia's decision to strike out on her own. The time passed quickly. When Kaia finally stopped talking to take a drink from a puddle, Scruff was surprised to find that he was feeling more alert than before.

"So, now you know my life story. What about yours?" Kaia asked, grinning.

Scruff shared a few things about his past, although he didn't talk about Pica much. It was easier not to. Kaia had lots of questions about the city, as she had never been there. Her eyes widened at his descriptions of sky trains and miles and miles of roads and pavement. While they talked, the rain stopped, and the moon came out.

Kaia took over again, telling more stories from her puppyhood. In the middle of one story about how her brothers and sisters had fought over every last bite of food, she caught him yawning.

"Sorry," he said quickly.

"Oh, don't worry. You look tired. That bush you chose isn't a really great place to nap. Want me to show you a better spot?"

He followed her to a cement wall that held back the dirt and plants along the slope down to the ocean. At one end was a large tree, and between the roots and the wall was a small depression in the ground. Scruff immediately caught sight of the spot and slid underneath a root to curl up in the hole. It was the perfect size. Warm, safe dirt surrounded him.

"Nice, huh?"

"I like it," he replied, peering out at her. "Thanks for the tip. And for the chat."

"It's nothing. I love to talk. I'm going to head out now. I usually hang out at another park on the other side of that busy road up there. It was nice to meet you. Hope to see you around."

"Thanks," Scruff repeated awkwardly. He watched her go, a slim, graceful figure. He tucked his nose under his tail, and for the first time in days, felt the warm world around him. He fell asleep listening to the soft shushing of the waves.

TWELVE

FRIEND

When Scruff woke, he felt disoriented, hearing a rhythmic rushing sound. After a moment, his brain connected it to the ocean. Looking through the tree roots, he saw that the sky was just beginning to lighten, and the moon was setting over the water.

He scraped along on his belly until he was out of the hollow, then had a deep stretch, grunting at his stiffness. Next, he turned his attention to his empty stomach. He stood for a moment on the beach, undecided. He could hunt along the train tracks and then return to this hollow on the beach for the day. Or, he could look for the park to say hello to Kaia. The thought of spending another long day completely alone spurred his feet over the train tracks and to the edge of the road. Although it was not fully daytime, there were already many cars travelling on it. If he waited much longer, it would be impassable.

He crouched, watching the steady stream of cars and waiting for the right moment. Eventually, he could hear and feel a gap coming; there was less vibration under his paws, and the sound of the cars lightened a little. Now relying on his sense of vision, he looked for his opportunity. There was the gap. He raced across, his claws skittering on the wet pavement. A honk split his ears and then he was across. His body felt very alive, as it always did after a tricky crossing. Now, to find the park.

On this side of the road, the area was residential, with roads, houses, and alleys. He stuck to the alleys, as humans were starting to wake up and begin their day. He had only a few minutes to find the park before full daylight hit and he'd have to wait under a bush for the day. He turned right and left, making increasingly wider circles outward from the place where he'd crossed the road, looking for some sign of a break between the houses.

He passed a gas station with its familiar oily smell and skirted around the back, where there were some scrubby bushes. He noticed a stand of tall trees rising up behind the gas station fence. Locating a well-worn hole in it, he smelled Kaia, confirming he was on the right track. On the other side of the fence was a small, square park with a few trees and a lot of grass. Bushes ringed the perimeter of the park, and at the side next to the road were a few swings. The other sides were bordered by fences with houses behind them. It was just like many he'd seen in the city.

Looking around, he spotted a young coyote — not Kaia — standing between two bushes on the opposite side of the park. Scruff froze. Then he saw the coyote wag his tail and flick his ears a few times. Friendly. Scruff exhaled with relief. He approached cautiously.

"Hey," said the other coyote. They both took a minute to circle and smell each other.

"Hi," Scruff replied. "I'm looking for Kaia."

"Oh, she just left. She'll be back soon. I'm heading out, too. You can stay here." With that, he turned and trotted off. Strange. Not unfriendly, but not really friendly, either. Still, with daylight coming, Scruff didn't want to take his chances outside of the park. He found cover under some bushes and lay down to wait.

It wasn't long before Kaia came loping across the park. She looked relaxed and happy. He stood up, and she spotted him, wagging her tail and coming over.

"It's cool you found me again. I didn't think you would," she said with a smile.

"Well, I was just passing by and thought I'd say hi." Scruff shifted his weight between his front paws. The smell of food emanated from her — she must have just eaten. His stomach growled loudly, making them both laugh.

"I see you could use some food. Want me to show you our secret? I think it's still early enough in the evening."

"Our?" Scruff was curious about her relationship to the other coyote he'd seen.

"Yeah, Casperandnoodleandchica."

"Huh?" She talked fast, and none of that last word made sense to Scruff.

87

"Casper's my best friend. Noodle and Chica hang out here, too. But those aren't really their names. I just started calling them that one day and it stuck. You'll have to meet them, then you'll understand."

"I see." Scruff wasn't exactly sure how to reply. He didn't have a lot of experience with new coyotes and had never heard such strange names.

"So, you want food or what?"

"Uh, sure." Scruff really did want some food and was curious about where the good hunting was around here, but he wasn't quite sure why she was being so friendly.

"Follow me."

Kaia headed back out the way Scruff had come in, flitting through the hole in the fence to the back of the gas station. She led him straight to the back of the building, where there was a small attached house with a front door and a porch. She walked brazenly up to the door and scratched it. She turned her head to grin at Scruff. "Watch this."

Scruff's body went into high alert as heavy footsteps approached the door. When it opened, he dove into the bushes, peering out in confusion. A small old woman stood there. Meanwhile, Kaia had completely transformed, sitting down with her tail wagging and her ears alert. The woman spoke kindly to Kaia, then disappeared back into the house. Kaia waited while Scruff just stared, his eyes wide. He couldn't believe Kaia was putting herself in such danger. A moment later, the woman returned and threw a big piece of food to Kaia, who gave a gentle woof and picked it up.

"Come on," she mumbled around the food in her mouth, leading him back to the park. Once there, she dropped the food onto the ground, and Scruff lowered his snout to smell it. Meat, but with something earthy and spicy. It smelled good. Maybe not as good as a rat or a fresh blackberry, but good.

"Go ahead, all yours. I already ate today. Isn't she amazing? We call her Friend."

Scruff looked at her, his mouth gaping. How was this okay? "But ..." He trailed off.

Kaia laughed. "I know, I used to be afraid, too. But I think there are bad humans and good humans. She's a good one. We've been taking her food for a long time now, and she's never done anything to hurt us. Go on, try it."

Scruff heard Pica's voice in his head, telling him to be wary of humans and their food. Then his stomach chimed in with a loud grumble. He pushed aside his unease and dug into the food. He would eat now and figure everything out later.

THIRTEEN
FEAST

A month later, Scruff was lying in the park, soaking up the weak spring sun and sleeping off a big meal, happy that all the humans had left so they had the park to themselves. Noodle and Chica were roughhousing in the bushes, yelping sharply whenever one nipped the other a bit too hard. Casper lay under his customary bush on the other side of the park. Kaia was off exploring somewhere but would probably be back soon.

Scruff stretched out, groaning at his full stomach. How had he found himself here? At first, he'd continued to scour the city for Pica, only visiting the park for short periods. He'd met Noodle and Chica and gotten to know Casper better. Each time he visited to be greeted with wagging tails, he felt the other threads of his life loosen a little. Being around them made him feel happy, and Kaia's enthusiasm and friendship slowly encircled him. Nowadays, he left the park less and less, and he'd inserted himself into the hierarchy of the pack.

They weren't a family pack, but they did have a hierarchy: Kaia was at the top, then Casper, then Noodle and Chica. Scruff was pretty much in the middle. He could easily beat Noodle and Chica when they roughhoused. Casper was aloof, but not aggressive; they mainly avoided each other. Being with this pack didn't patch the hole in his heart left by Pica, but it did distract him so he thought of her less and less.

The only thing that bothered him was their love of human food. Scruff had never in his life hunted so little, yet been so well fed. He did still hunt from time to time because it felt wrong to depend completely on Friend for food, but he was getting lazier by the day. He didn't go to Friend's door himself, but he did now stand in the open when she gave food to Kaia.

Hunting less also meant he had more time to play. He loved interacting with coyotes his own age. Jagger had mostly left him alone as a pup, and with Pica, it was just the two of them. Here, he was constantly getting pounced on, having his tail pulled, and rolling around on the grass with the others. He felt himself grow stronger by the day from all the roughhousing.

Kaia was always playing tricks on him, sneaking up and dropping pine cones on his head. She was interesting to talk to because she pushed him to explain himself and debated things he took for granted. The only source of tension between them was the subject of food. Scruff kept trying to tell her they should rely less on Friend, and Kaia kept asking for a good reason why. When Scruff told her how humans had destroyed his home and captured Pica, Kaia just repeated that some were bad and some were good. "And anyway," she would always say, "that was in the city. Here, things are relaxed."

These conversations were mostly lighthearted, but Scruff was becoming frustrated. She wouldn't listen to him. Even worse, if he kept on trying to hammer his point home, she'd just get up and go talk to Casper, and then their laughter would filter across the park back to Scruff. He realized he was going to have to change his strategy.

One night, as dusk fell, he watched Kaia and Casper talking quietly, lying side by side. They had been spending more time together in the past few days. What could Scruff do to get Kaia to hang out with him? He looked around for inspiration. A squirrel chattered at him from the base of a tree. A current ran through his body, and his mouth watered.

"Kaia!" he called out. "Come on an adventure with me tonight."

She turned to him and wagged her tail. "What kind of adventure?"

"I'll tell you when we get there."

Laughing, she stood up and stretched. "Okay, you got me."

"Let's go get some food from Friend," Casper said, sounding annoyed.

Kaia nosed him. "I'm not hungry right now. You go, and I'll catch up with you later."

Casper looked surprised, and Scruff felt a rush of energy. He stretched deeply and then hopped up, his tail wagging so hard it made his entire rear end move from side to side.

"All right, follow me!"

As they set out, a light snow began to fall, the soft flakes illuminated by streetlights, melting as soon as they touched the pavement. The streets felt magical, especially as it hadn't snowed in a month. Scruff led the way, winding downhill, sticking to alleyways and greenways. Kaia's paws padded softly behind him. They didn't speak, but their silence was comfortable.

Finally, they reached a major street. A fence ran along the far side, with a big open space behind it. They waited until there were no cars, then darted across. Scruff headed straight for a broken section of fence, and they quickly squeezed through. Sniffing carefully, he determined that they were the only ones there.

"Whoa," Kaia gasped. "How did you find this place?"

The land dropped sharply in front of them, revealing a long grassy hill with a building at the bottom. Beyond the building, the lights of the bridge twinkled over the water. The whole area smelled like animals, fresh hay, and human food, but right now, nothing moved. It was so different from the surrounding human houses — a hidden, delightful surprise.

"Do you like it?"

"I love it!"

93

Scruff gestured to the lights. "That land over there is where Pica and I came from."

"Do you ever want to go back? Do you miss it? And her?"

He hesitated. He'd told Kaia a lot more about his past, but still hadn't gotten into why he and Pica had fought. He'd just told her that they had decided to go their separate ways. Despite this, he tried to be as honest as possible in his answer. "I used to, a lot. But right now" — he glanced at her sitting tall beside him, her fur waving with the breeze — "I'm feeling pretty good about being here."

They both stared straight ahead for a while, comfortable not talking. Then Kaia jumped up. "Can we explore?"

"Of course. I brought you here because it's a great spot to catch mice. Down by that building, there are so many rodents you can't even walk without stepping on one!" Kaia didn't answer, but she slowed down. He glanced at her, unable to read her expression. "But keep an eye out for other coyotes. This is a popular spot."

He took off down the hill. As they approached the building, he lightened his tread. Wanting Kaia to experience the magic of hunting, he slowed to let her pass him. One careful paw at a time, she stalked toward the edge of the building, where there was a cart, some hay, and a stack of large crates. His ears twitched, and his mouth watered. He could hear dozens of mice stamping their tiny feet and squeaking.

Kaia moved gracefully, her body low to the ground. A few times, she froze, listening intently. Finally, she reached the pile of hay. One more step, then two, and she was right against it. For a moment, she was a statue, only her sides moving in and out gently. Then she sprang into the air and landed in the middle of the hay. Scruff bounded over.

"Dang." She scowled. "That mouse was right there. How did it get away?"

The rest of the mice, now alerted, had gone silent or fled. Scruff bumped Kaia gently. "It's okay, there are lots of other spots. Let's try again."

"Okay." She sounded hesitant. "Or we could just head back and relax in the grass, then get food from Friend."

Scruff wasn't ready to give up yet. "One more try, at least."

"All right."

They spent a long time prowling around, trying to catch a mouse. After three failed attempts, Kaia said she was tired. Scruff left her to rest and caught his own mouse. He carried it back proudly, but Kaia just ate it quickly, without a word. As they left the grassy lot and slowly wound their way back through the dark streets, she talked about how much she was looking forward to Friend's food. Irritation rose in Scruff's chest, but he pushed it down, wanting to enjoy the time with her.

The others were happy to see them, especially Casper. He placed his head over Kaia's neck, pushing on her playfully. "Did you catch anything?"

"Not really. We didn't actually hunt much. Scruff showed me a cool spot, though."

Scruff curled up nearby, his mind unsettled. It had been a lovely evening, but until tonight, he'd had no idea how little hunting his new friends actually did. It had been a mouse paradise tonight, yet Kaia couldn't catch a single one. And he'd never seen any of the others catch a rodent, either. They snacked on bark, plants, and insects, but their main food source was Friend.

Despite his unease, as more time passed, Scruff found himself drawing closer to Kaia. He began to hunt less and hang out with her more, and she started napping next to him rather than with Casper. That felt so good that Scruff found himself following her rhythm. He missed hunting, but that was balanced by his joy at feeling a close bond again. He still suggested hunting missions sometimes, but usually out of boredom, not hunger.

One late afternoon, a rough tongue scraped the side of his face, waking him from a light nap. He wagged his tail a little, rolling over to greet Kaia with a smile.

"Thinking deep thoughts?" she joked. "Lost in planning how to catch your next mouse?"

"What's up, Kaia?"

"Guess what!"

"What?"

"You're supposed to guess!" She poked him playfully with her nose.

"Okay … you found a new Dumpster filled with fried chicken."

"Nope, guess again."

"Just tell me!"

"Too easy."

"Uh … you found a better park."

She smiled, her head cocked and her nose scrunched.

"Fine, I'll tell you. Friend left a bunch of boxes outside her door filled with food and other things! Come back with me and have some. It'll probably be chewed over by mice and other animals by dark."

The sun was beaming down brightly. Kaia sounded confident, but even she rarely showed herself to humans in full daylight. Scruff hesitated, a weird feeling rippling through him.

"I'm not that hungry." Seeing her narrow her eyes, he quickly added, "Sounds cool, though. I'll check it out tonight."

"Scruff, you're always hungry. You're just too scared to go!"

He felt his hackles rise and took a deep breath, trying to relax them. "I just don't feel like it. I'm not scared."

"Are, too. Come on, I'll go with you," Kaia yipped, turning a full circle of excitement.

Scruff couldn't think of an excuse. "Okay, but just a quick trip."

Kaia shook out her coat. "That's the spirit! Chica! Noodle! Casper! Mission starting!"

Noodle poked his nose out of the bushes. "Now?"

"Yes, a huge food stash. Now or never."

Scruff got up as Noodle and Chica trotted over, a spring in their steps. Kaia barked again at Casper, who grunted from the other side of the park, "Still digesting. Have fun."

"You are going to die when you see this!" Kaia danced back and forth in excitement. They followed her through the park, under the old fence, and around the back of the building. The gas station was busy, and all the human smells and sounds made Scruff's stomach turn. At the back door, they were out of sight of the cars, but someone could walk around the side of the building at any moment.

Boxes of every size and shape were piled outside the door. Big garbage bags were strewn across the pavement, many of them split open. The others dove in immediately, but Scruff took his time, investigating each bag and box. Most contained food, but some contained other human objects. He sniffed cautiously, unsure how safe they were.

When he found a box that smelled like salty fish, however, he couldn't help himself. He began to gorge, tearing open packages and wolfing down the food. Soon, he felt his belly pushing against his ribs. Chica was sprawled on the pavement, smiling at Noodle as he pulled weird things out of boxes to show her. Kaia paced slowly, looking relaxed. She caught Scruff's eye. "Ready to go back now? A little less hungry?"

"You'll have to roll me home," Scruff replied with a smile. He felt instant relief as they slid under the fence back to the quiet of the park. There, he didn't feel so exposed and could focus on digesting the mass of food in his stomach.

"You're welcome." Kaia laughed as they all groaned and curled up under a bush. "You can thank me when you're old and fat." She lay with her head close to Scruff's, searching his eyes for a minute. "It still makes you nervous, doesn't it?"

"I don't know. I don't quite understand it."

"What do you mean?" She frowned.

Scruff hated himself for not being able to just enjoy the moment. "I don't know how to explain it," he confessed. "I guess I'm just new to all of this, and I have to get used to it." He hesitated. "Thanks. I feel good."

Kaia shook her head and curled up next to him. A minute later, her breathing slowed as she sank into sleep. Scruff rested his head on his paws, his mind spinning. He loved his new friends, especially Kaia, but he still couldn't shake the feeling that something was wrong. Pica had been so angry at him when he'd stolen the bread from the truck. And compared to this, that had been nothing. What would she say if she could him now? Something inside him hardened, and he pushed the thought of her away. She had chosen to leave him. He had figured out his life, and she could figure out hers. It wasn't his problem anymore.

PART FOUR
DECISIONS

FOURTEEN
BADGER

Pica

After her traumatic paw injury, Pica had spent several weeks lounging by the river, healing and watching this new coyote pack. Getting back to the city was never far from her mind, but she had found some peace in the fact that there was nothing she could do for now except let herself heal. She found herself settling into a new rhythm. With such a large pack, there was always someone around to keep her company. They taught her something about this new environment each day — information she would need if she wanted to make it on her own. Rip and Rooney had made it their personal goal to keep her entertained, always finding some way to make her laugh. She goofed around with them both, but found that she really enjoyed talking to Rooney in particular. When Rip wasn't around to push him and nip at him, he was quiet and thoughtful, telling her all kinds of stories about the land around them and his adventures hunting.

Back when she had first escaped from the truck, she'd found much here to be strange. But not until she heard Rooney's stories had she realized just how different her life in the city and in the Wild Lands was from theirs. Rooney had explained that his pack often hunted together to catch larger animals, like deer. Pica had seen many deer before and had eaten deer meat when she had found it already dead, she had never even considered catching one. Rooney had also told her all that they occasionally entered human territory — though they stayed far away from the houses — to hunt other animals. One in particular, a kind of sheep, was not especially quick or agile, but its thick, woolly coat actually made it hard to catch. A few times last winter, when food was scarce, the pack had taken a sheep.

Another difference Pica had noticed was how much larger these coyotes were than what she was used to. They smelled like city coyotes and sounded like city coyotes, but even those the same age as her, like Rip and Rooney, were broader and taller. They must have to be bigger in order to contend with all of the serious challenges out here. Rooney had told her there were other kinds of human traps besides leg traps, and also that humans could point a kind of big stick from a distance and, with a very loud bang, kill a coyote without even coming close or touching it.

Pica had been horrified and wondered if any humans in the city had these things.

Rooney had also talked about his mother, Leila, who had been the alpha of the pack for many years. She was tough, he said, and had suffered many losses. So many of her pups had died, as had her partner, Arnou. She was getting old now, and he thought maybe Bruno would take over one day soon.

One morning, Rooney raced back from a hunt, panting, with a rodent in his mouth for her. "All right, Pica, eat this and then let's go!" It was midmorning, and Pica's brain still hadn't fully adjusted to their high level of activity in the daytime. Her family had always hunted at night, then slumbered and relaxed all day. Here, it was upside down. The coyotes slept for most of the night, instead hunting at dawn, dusk, and really at any time during the day. This must be possible because there were barely any humans around. In fact, Pica discovered that she actually liked the rhythm of the day being this way. Snuggling between warm bodies was a good way to stay warm at night, and it was fun to be up while the sun was shining.

The morning was warm, with sunlight filtering in through the trees. As Rooney pranced away, the idea of an adventure thrilled Pica. She had been stuck at the creek for so long. And if she wanted to get back to the Wild Lands, she'd have to start somewhere. She gulped down the mouse and followed Rooney across the small creek to the meadow behind it. She limped, putting as little weight on her paw as possible. After a couple months of healing, it didn't hurt anymore, but it didn't work like it used to, either. She was worried about tripping.

Small, bright wildflowers dotted the grass. Birds trilled, and a gentle breeze blew across the open space. Snuffling along with her nose to the ground, she delighted in all the smells. Suddenly, Rooney hip checked her, knocking her over, and raced away.

"What the …?" Pica smiled. Playing like this felt so normal. She tucked her bad paw up to her chest and awkwardly began to chase him. It took a few strides to find her balance, adjusting where she placed her front paw to centre it underneath her, but soon she was picking up speed, her claws digging into the soft grass and dirt. Wind whipped her fur, and she almost felt free.

Rooney stopped on the far side of the meadow and turned to watch her. "Not bad! How does it feel?"

"It's really hard to hold my leg. But this feels pretty good."

"Want to try hunting?"

Pica's good mood evaporated. "Nope. Let's just keep running in the sun."

Rooney cocked his head to the side, studying her. "You scared?"

"You know as well as I do that I won't be able to hunt. I don't want to think about it."

He opened his mouth, then seemed to change his mind. "Come with me. There's someone I want you to meet."

Pica frowned. Hadn't she met everyone in the pack already? "It's not a wolf, is it? You have a bad habit of running into them."

"Wolves don't hang out around here," Rooney responded breezily. "Not usually," he added, smiling back over his shoulder.

Pica shook her head. "Who is it? Tell me!"

They wound through a small stand of trees, following an old deer trail. Pica's leg muscles were burning, but she refused to complain. This was the first time in weeks that she'd been outside the creek area. Rooney stopped often to sniff, apparently looking for a particular scent. He got excited as he entered the edge of a large open field, and let out a sharp bark. A chorus of ground squirrels squeaked angrily and promptly disappeared into their holes.

"Is that it? You're showing me all of the ground squirrels I can't eat?" Pica smiled. The squirrels were fat and tempting, but almost impossible to catch. Their incredible underground tunnels made it easy for them get away.

"Just wait." Rooney barked again.

Then, in the middle of the field, a black-and-white-striped head popped up between clumps of bright-green grass and let out a grunt. Pica stared in astonishment — was it a skunk? She took a step back.

"Hey!" Rooney barked again, and the odd thing started to shuffle toward them. "It's my friend Bodi. He's a badger."

"A badger?"

"Yep. I met him last summer. I can't really understand what he's saying — he just grunts — but he's pretty fun to hunt with."

The badger was close now, his black eyes fixed on Pica. His face was striped with white, from his nose to behind his little, round ears. The rest of his small, fat body was a mottled grey. His ears wiggled gently as he surveyed them both. He nodded and grunted again, then turned his back on them, stretching deeply. Without sparing another look, he waddled off toward the middle of the field.

"Friendly guy," Pica muttered.

"You'll see. Stay here and watch," Rooney said cheerfully. He walked parallel to the badger, a short distance away. Bodi seemed to be in no rush, sniffing the ground-squirrel holes as he went along. He stopped at one of them and pawed at the entrance. Pica walked quietly to the top of a small knoll nearer the opening so she could see better. Without fanfare, Bodi started digging furiously, his strong front paws sweeping dirt away at an incredible pace. He occasionally used his back paws to keep the area clear. Rooney hovered a few feet away, his body tense.

Pica was staring hard at the digging badger when she sensed a swift movement in the corner of her eye and looked over to see that Rooney had a ground squirrel in his mouth. He shook it triumphantly and brought it over to Pica. "Check it out! You have this one. We're going to keep going."

Pica frowned, not sure what had happened exactly. But she gratefully began to eat the ground squirrel, looking up frequently to check on what Rooney and Bodi were doing. Moving in tandem across the field as angry ground squirrels kept close track of where they were, they were working together. Sometimes Rooney would chase a squirrel into its hole, then Bodi would quickly dig into the earth, catching it. Sometimes Bodi would dig in one area, scaring a squirrel right out of a different hole, where Rooney quietly waited at the entrance. It looked like hard work, and they did miss quite a few, but in the course of an hour, each of them caught at least a couple of the rodents. Pica watched it all in amazement.

Eventually, Rooney tired, and he barked at Bodi, who grunted back, then disappeared back into the grass. Rooney joined Pica and lay down in the sun.

"How did you meet Bodi? How did you figure all this out?" Pica demanded.

"My mom showed me. I guess sometimes it's better for both of us to hunt together. Isn't it fun?"

"It's amazing. I've never seen anything like it."

Rooney looked at her joyfully. "See? There are lots of different ways to hunt. Like when the whole pack hunts a deer. Not everyone has to be strong alone. We're strong together."

"I know, I used to hunt with —" Pica stopped. She didn't want to talk about Scruff. If she did, she would have to face the reality that in a few weeks, she was setting off to try to get back to the city, even if it killed her. She'd promised herself. "With my family," she finished.

"You really miss your family, don't you?" Rooney asked with concern.

"Yes."

"I'm sorry. I don't know what I would do without mine." He looked up at the sky. "We should head back now. It's getting late."

The afternoon fun had ended. Pica stood up. Her good legs felt sore from the exercise, but she wasn't too stiff as she trotted back. Maybe Leila was right — maybe she did have a shot at completing the journey. But when the time came, would she have the courage to leave? She would have to say goodbye to her new friends, pass through wolf territory, and cross over the ice mountains, all in the hopes that if she did make it to the city, she could find Scruff. And if she did find him … would he still be waiting for her?

Pushing these thoughts from her mind, she concentrated on getting back to the creek without falling on her face.

FIFTEEN
MOVING DAY

Scruff

The evening after they went through the boxes behind the gas station, Scruff followed Kaia and the others to see if there was any food left. The mess they'd left had been cleaned up, and Friend didn't answer the door when Kaia scratched. Kaia cocked her head to the side, but brushed it off when Scruff asked if she was worried. "Nope. She goes away from time to time. I guess we'll have to find food somewhere else tonight."

They picked through the boxes again and got what they could, but soon left to scavenge in the alleys. For fun, Scruff hunted some mice. When he caught one, Kaia laughed. "You just worked for the last half hour to catch that tiny little morsel, and meanwhile I've had all kinds of snacks."

"But it's delicious! Why don't you practise with me tonight?"

"Why don't we get some more snacks from the Dumpster over here and then head back to the park to hang out with everyone else?"

"It could be fun," he insisted, poking her with his nose.

"Scruff, I've been thinking about this a lot. The strongest coyotes get the most food with the least amount of effort or risk. It's all about being efficient. In our case, getting food from Friend is the best way to survive. I'm sure she'll be back soon. We won't starve in the meantime. You can hunt if you want, but I'm going to head back."

Scruff's body was tingling. The darkness and the cold air surrounding him made him feel alive. "I'm going to stick around here for a while longer. See you back at the park later."

"Okay. Have fun!" Kaia laughed as she trotted off.

Scruff watched her go. He felt equal pull and push with Kaia. Her positive energy pulled him in, and she had a way of making him feel truly happy. However, something was holding him back from fully committing to their friendship. He could never quite read her. That laugh — had it been friendly, or a bit mocking?

Rather than dwell on the question, he shook his fur out and tuned into his surroundings. It was the middle of the night, and few humans were out. He could hear a few cars driving in the distance, and a dog barked somewhere far away, but for the most part, it was remarkably peaceful. He spent the next few hours wandering and exploring, losing track of time as he quietly slipped down alleys and caught rodents. He kept it up until his belly felt heavy, then he began his slow lope back to the park. Proud of himself for getting enough food on his own by hunting, he was looking forward to seeing his friends again.

That feeling evaporated when he got back to the park and looked for Kaia. Rather than waiting for him under their usual bush, she was curled up next to Casper. Casper lifted his head gently, his tail wagging, but his eyes weren't all that friendly. Kaia slept on. Scruff wagged his tail in return and quickly turned away. He curled up by himself, feeling cold and confused.

The next night, once again, Friend did not come out. By now, her smells were stale. It was clear that she hadn't been outside in days, and Scruff sensed that she was gone. Kaia tossed her head and headed out with Chica to find human trash in the alleys, but they came back still hungry. That next day, they all talked about how much they were looking forward to Friend's return.

"She's done this before — gone away for a while and then come back. And she always gives us the best stuff when she comes back," Kaia explained to Scruff.

The third night, Friend was still gone, but the following morning, a large truck backed onto the pavement beside her front door, loudly beeping and clunking. The coyotes raced to the hole in the fence and peered through. Noodle began drooling with excitement. "She brought a whole truck of food for us!"

However, no one unloaded any food. A few humans jumped out of the truck and proceeded to bring boxes out from inside the house, loading them in the truck. Scruff glanced at Kaia and saw unease on her face before she replaced it with her usual air of nonchalance. "Interesting," she said. "Well, let's leave it for today and go back tonight to see."

That night, they all trooped back to Friend's house. The surrounding area was now empty. The cold wind whipped across the pavement, and Scruff shivered. After a few moments, they headed back to the park, silent.

Kaia seemed to recover. "All right. Who wants to come with me to a sweet Dumpster I found recently?"

Casper jumped up immediately. "Sure. Let's go!"

Noodle and Chica shook their heads. "We'll relax here for a bit," said Chica. "We'll keep an eye on Friend's place to see if anything changes."

"Scruff?" Kaia asked, already heading out with Casper.

"I'm good. I'll go do some hunting on my own."

Scruff stayed out for a few hours, appreciating the slightly warmer weather and the full moon guiding him through the streets. When he returned to the park, the others were already back.

Casper was lying under a bush, groaning. "Ohhh … I shouldn't have eaten that weird stuff."

Noodle laughed. "That's on you, Casper. If it's weird smelling, don't eat it! You know that."

"But I was so hungry!"

"It'll pass."

"Why don't you eat some mice?" Scruff asked. "Mice don't make your stomach hurt."

The other coyotes turned to look at him. Casper narrowed his eyes, lifting his head higher. "Easy for you to say, Hunter. We haven't done that in a long time now."

"Don't stress so much, Scruff," Kaia added. "Casper's fine. He's just got a weak stomach, right?" She leaned over and poked him in the side with her nose. The tension was broken, and they all went back to lying down. Scruff curled up alone under a bush.

A week later, new humans moved into the house. After the big truck had been unloaded and had left, the coyotes all gathered outside, tucking themselves into the bushes to watch the door. The soft evening light cast long shadows. They could hear the humans inside. Kaia was the first to move. Trembling, she slunk up to the door and scratched. Scruff held his breath. Several minutes passed. Nothing happened.

Then she yipped once, loudly, and scratched again. It seemed at first as though no one would come. Then they heard footsteps, and a woman opened the door. She was larger than Friend and smelled very different. Wonderful, delicious smells of food being cooked wafted out along with her. Scruff started to drool.

The woman looked down at Kaia and froze. As usual, Kaia wagged her tail gently, looking as friendly as possible. The woman let out a piercing shriek and slammed the door. Kaia jumped back, surprised. A few seconds later, a man opened the door and threw something large at her. There was a deep thunk as it hit her in the side, and she yelped. Immediately, they all fled back to the park. Kaia was limping slightly, clearly in pain.

"Well," she announced, wincing, "it looks like we'll have to find another human." She sat down, her head hanging low. "I wish I wasn't so hungry — I need to think." The others just looked at her. Their fearless leader had reached a wall she wasn't sure how to get over.

After a few minutes, she got up and headed over to a bush. "I don't feel like going out right now. That thing really hurt! I think we should rest for now. We can go out and look for more food in a bit."

The others nodded their assent. Scruff felt hungry and restless, though. "I think I'll go look for some food. Anyone want to join me?" He looked from one coyote to the next, but they all avoided his gaze.

Casper finally spoke up. "We'll hang here with Kaia to make sure she's okay. We'll probably hit some garbage bins later."

"I guess I'll see you later." As Scruff headed out, he realized just how much sway Kaia held over this straggly group of coyotes. He hadn't fully understood before tonight that her lead was so strong, whatever she did, the rest would follow.

When he returned the next morning, he was surprised to see the group's spirits had completely changed. Noodle and Chica were play fighting, and Casper and Kaia were talking together with excitement.

"Did you see how surprised he was?" Kaia exclaimed, laughing.

"You were so fast, like lightning!" Casper replied, touching her softly with his nose. Scruff stiffened and walked over slowly.

"What's up? What did I miss?"

"Scruff, you missed a crazy night! Casper and I set out a little while ago to find some food, and we found a group of humans at another park not far from here. It was a bit weird, because they almost never hang out in the middle of the night, but I guess they're out more now that it's spring. Anyway, they were being really loud, so they didn't even notice me when —"

Casper cut in eagerly. "She leapt up and grabbed a bag right off the table in front of them! It was so easy. They didn't notice until we were on the other side of their park. We ran and ran, and then we hid and ate the food in the bag. And man, it was so good!" He paused. "We probably should have saved you, some, hey? Well, you can come with us next time."

Scruff just stared at them. He had understood taking food from humans when it was offered, but stealing it right out from under their noses? He'd never heard anything like it. "That's dangerous, guys!" he said with rising panic. "Stealing food that way — you definitely shouldn't do that again."

Kaia looked at him with her soft brown eyes. "Don't worry, okay? The idea that humans are dangerous is just a myth. They're slow, they can't see in the dark, and their hearing and sense of smell must be terrible, because they didn't notice us at all. It's fine if you don't want to join us yet, but you'll see. This is going to work out great for everyone."

What was she talking about? Scruff tried to act normal, but nervous energy was buzzing inside of him, and he just couldn't keep listening to her. He couldn't find the words to express what he was feeling.

Noodle and Chica had stopped playing and wandered over. "And I'll get something for you tomorrow, Noodle," Chica bragged. "You know I'm faster than you."

"We'll see about that!" Noodle replied, knocking her hard and starting the play again. Clearly, everyone was relieved that they had a new plan. Scruff joined in, but he couldn't quite relax and enjoy it.

SIXTEEN
DECISION

Pica

As spring wore on, the poplar and scrub oak trees that bordered the creek unfurled their bright-green leaves, completely transforming the area. The ground was no longer hard and frozen, and it smelled delightfully alive. In the land around the creek, there was even more activity. Baby rodents were born, squeaking and scurrying under bushes. Leila's coyote pack found food more easily, working together to hunt young deer and munching the fresh shoots of plants. The days got longer, and each day, Pica got a little stronger.

She had a much better understanding of injuries now. Getting attacked by the big cat had been very scary and painful, but most of the cuts had been shallow, and no muscles or joints had been injured. Her wounds had been sore for a few weeks, but had healed, leaving only some thin scars down her back and sides. She had previously injured her leg fighting Jagger on her family's hillside, but that time, she'd also been very sick — hot, weak, moving in and out of consciousness. This time, after escaping the trap and suffering a few weeks of pain and throbbing, her paw felt relatively normal. She wasn't able to run with her full weight on the injured leg, but she could stand without pain. Not all injuries were equal. She was glad this one was healing up well enough for her to function.

She went out every day, spending more and more time with the pack. Her good front leg became strong and muscled, and she learned to tuck her bad leg up against her body when she was in a full sprint. She wasn't as fast as she had been before and would fall behind, but at least she was able to find joy in running again, feeling the wind whip through her fur, stretching her tail out behind her for balance.

As the weather got warmer, Pica began to think about leaving. Each day, when she woke, she'd stand up and stretch, wondering if this would be the right day to take off. Then, the warmth of the sun and the playfulness of the pack would lull her into waiting just one more day. So much time had passed already — what was another day? Especially since she would be a little stronger tomorrow. No one from the pack brought up the subject, but she knew they were thinking about it, too.

Her upcoming departure hung in the air, unsaid at all times.

One particularly warm day, when most of the other coyotes were out alone or in pairs, hunting and exploring, Pica returned early and sought the shade, not something she usually did at midday.

Leila approached and wagged her tail gently in greeting. She joined Pica in the shade of the tree. "Nice day," she woofed as she circled slowly, looking for the perfect patch of dirt to lie down in.

"Yes, spring is definitely here." Pica kept her voice casual, but she wondered if Leila had really come over to exchange banalities. She had never done so before.

There was a long silence. Pica looked up to see that Leila was studying her carefully. Her heart started racing. Had she done something wrong? Was she going to be asked to leave?

"You like it here," Leila began carefully. Her expression was unreadable. "You fit in well with our pack. The others like having you around. And you're doing very well with your injury. I'm so glad it's healed well."

"Me, too." Where was she going with this? Pica waited, her eyes downcast and her heart thumping against her chest.

"I remember that when you first arrived, I couldn't hold you back from leaving," Leila continued. "Now, I'm not sure what it is that you want. You are welcome to stay here. I think Rooney wants you to stay. But I wonder, if you did stay, would you always wonder what became of your old life?"

Pica was unsure how to respond, but finally decided to be truthful. "You're right, I don't quite know what I want anymore."

"I can understand that. But you should know that I think you're strong enough to leave now. I see it in the way you run and hunt with us. You know so much more than you did when you arrived. If you do plan to leave, make sure you don't wait too long. That will only make leaving more difficult."

Discomfort welled up in Pica. She had, in fact, been delaying her decision, using her injury as an excuse. "I'm sorry, I never meant to stay here so long. It's just ... I'm scared to leave. What if I step into another trap or run into the wolves again?"

The other coyotes were starting to return. Leila stood and stretched. "There's no need to be sorry. It's your decision to stay or go; I accept it either way. But I don't think you should make the decision out of fear or put it off any longer. Think deeply about what you want to do and then commit to it. Staying too long in this middle space is dangerous." Her eyes held a gentle warning in them. She nodded at Pica and went off to meet the other coyotes. With gentle woofs and licks, they greeted each other.

Rooney trotted over, his tail wagging. "Pica, guess what happened this morning!"

It was painful for Pica to acknowledge how happy she was to see him. She managed a wan smile. "What?"

"Hey, what's wrong?"

"Nothing. It's just ... my leg hurts."

"Oh, I'm sorry." As Rooney bent to sniff it, Pica felt a pang of guilt. He was the one she was closest to, but he was the last one she could ask to help her make this decision.

She forced cheerfulness into her voice. "So, what happened?"

Rooney launched into a story about Rip chasing a rabbit. Though Pica faced him with her ears perked up, she didn't hear a word; her brain was elsewhere. Leila's words had really thrown her.

When Rooney was done telling the story, Rip came over to bother him for spreading the embarrassing story about the rabbit getting away. After a few pointed nose pokes and paw swipes, Rooney took the bait and leapt up, barking roughly at his brother. Then they were off, and Pica had some time alone again.

With no one watching her, she took the opportunity to leave the home base, following the creek uphill to where it entered the ground. There, she stopped at a green, grassy knoll with a view of the surrounding fields. The late afternoon sunlight lit up the grass, turning it translucent.

Pica sighed. The days had turned into months. Now it was early summer, and there was no reason to delay any further. It was just so hard to contemplate leaving the safety and happiness of this pack for an uncertain, dangerous journey. But as she lay there and forced herself to decide, she realized that she already knew what she would do. She had known from the moment Leila started talking to her that she was going to leave. An incredibly strong force was pulling her back to the Wild Lands.

She'd never fully be able to feel at home here; she'd always wonder what had happened to Scruff. She had to at least try to find out.

She heard footsteps coming up softly behind her. Rooney sat down next to her with an air of melancholy.

"You're leaving, aren't you?"

"How did you know?" Pica asked, surprised.

"My mom told me to find you. She said it was probably time."

Pica realized with awe just how wise Leila really was. She forced herself to meet Rooney's eyes. Sadness clouded his features.

"I'm sorry, Rooney. It's been so wonderful here. You helped me heal, and I'm so thankful. But I need to get back to my real home."

With a sigh, Rooney lay down. "I've never met anyone like you before. You're small and scrawny and injured, but you still go for the kill, just like the biggest coyote. If anyone can make it over those ice mountains, it's you." He paused, thinking. "Would you let me come with you to the foothills? I can help you make it through wolf territory."

"I don't want to put you into any danger," Pica replied.

"That's my decision."

She struggled internally for a moment. "Okay."

"When?" The tension in Rooney's voice betrayed his feelings.

"Tomorrow?" Pica phrased it as a question, even though she'd already made up her mind.

"Okay. We'd better rest well tonight."

"Rooney?"

"Yes?" He turned his dark-brown eyes on her. She almost forgot what she wanted to say. "Thanks for being such a good friend. I don't think I would have made it to this point without you."

"It wasn't completely selfless. I think you know that I like you."

Pica felt hot and uncomfortable. "I guessed."

"I'm still secretly hoping that you won't be able to make it over the mountains so you'll have to come back here. I'll wait a few months, in case."

She leaned over and placed her face next to his. "I'm sorry."

They lay in stillness for a while, listening to the stream bubbling out of the ground and cascading down the hillside behind them. In the far distance, a lone wolf howled.

SEVENTEEN
GUN

Scruff

Bright-yellow flowers had started to bloom all around
the park. Humans had started to come to use the playground more often, forcing the coyotes to spend longer
periods tucked away in the bushes during the daytime.
Scruff missed the days of living at the edge of the golf
course, where there had been wide-open space to lie out
in the sun, feeling the warmth bake his fur and relax his
muscles. In any case, it was nice to have a home.

Kaia and Casper had continued to steal food from
humans, often in broad daylight, since that was when
most humans were out and about. Noodle and Chica
were a bit more hesitant. They headed out in the early

evening, when it was less busy but still bright. Scruff found himself increasingly isolated, alone in the park during the day and hunting by himself at night. He still scavenged for human food in garbage cans, but he never approached the humans themselves. He had chosen this path, yet still, he felt a piercing sense of abandonment every time Kaia and Casper headed out, their jaunty tails wagging as they joked with each other. Day by day, they were becoming closer.

As good a hunter as Scruff had become, he was often hungry. When he lay in the park during the day, his stomach rumbling, he would think of the others out there eating human food. The long, lonely hours tested his resolve. A few times, he almost decided to join them, but his pride stopped him. They assumed that he was hunting for all of his meals, and he didn't want to admit that he couldn't always catch enough to satisfy his hunger.

One evening, after another long day on his own, Scruff felt the loneliness well up inside of him. Remembering when it had been normal to fear humans, he wished that Pica were there. He'd have loved to talk it all over with her.

His thoughts were distracted by a honking car horn, and then he spotted Kaia and Casper at the far side of the park.

"That was close!" he heard Casper exclaim. Kaia bumped him in reply. Seeing that simple gesture of friendship broke something inside Scruff. He felt so painfully alone.

"Hey, Scruff!" Kaia called out, trotting over to touch her nose to his. Scruff wagged his tail in reply. "Want to hear what we got up to tonight?"

"Sure," he said, although he really didn't.

Casper jumped in, his bark loud and excited. "We went inside a human house! It was crazy — they left their door open, and we walked right in." He paused at Scruff's shocked expression and tried to explain. "We sniffed pretty carefully and didn't think anyone was there. We just wondered what it was like."

"There was stuff everywhere," Kaia continued, picking up the story. "The ground was kind of like grass, but it smelled bad."

"Smelled bad?" Scruff couldn't quite imagine it.

"Well" — Kaia exchanged glances with Casper — "it's kind of hard to explain. Anyway, there was a room with so much food! We had to jump onto a kind of ledge to get at it, but it was amazing. The humans' places are stockpiled with food — and they don't even eat it all. They're even dumber than we thought!"

Scruff swallowed back a retort. "Wow," he replied. He couldn't think of anything else to say. Kaia and Casper lay down, and Scruff lay down next to them, listening to more of their breathless stories. He couldn't quite believe what they were saying, and yet he could see their swollen bellies under their fur. He didn't know how to react. Eventually, he turned over and pretended to fall asleep so they wouldn't see how confused he was.

By the next evening, Scruff had decided to try out a kind of compromise, a way that he and Kaia could find food together. With a plan in mind, he softly padded over to Kaia, who was cleaning herself under a tree.

"Hey, can I ask you a favour?"

"What is it?"

"Can you show me how to get human food? And in return, I'll show you how to catch a frog."

She tilted her head, studying him. "You want to find human food? Well, it's definitely easier in the daytime."

Scruff paused. "Of course. But you can show me some of your favourite spots, right? Even if there isn't anyone there now?"

"Sure, it could be fun. And I've never caught a frog before. Where can you find them?"

Scruff danced from paw to paw, excited that his plan was working. "I'll show you!"

"Okay." Kaia yawned, and dropped her head back onto her paws. She noticed him waiting there, his tail wagging, and smiled. "Oh, you mean right now! Okay, I guess now is good."

Worried she might change her mind, Scruff headed out swiftly. They were gone before any of the others even realized they were leaving. As they walked, they found small plant shoots and dug in the now-thawed ground for grubs and bugs. Kaia pointed out a few houses and parks where she had easily found human food. Soon they reached a small park with a little pond in the centre. The frogs there had recently come out of hibernation.

Scruff motioned to Kaia to follow him silently. The fading daylight was giving way to the moon rising. All around the pond, insects and frogs sang. He paused for a minute, savouring the stillness and being alone with Kaia. Then he slowly approached the edge of the pond, using his nose and ears to follow one particular frog song.

Seconds later, he pounced, catching the frog between his paws. Everything went silent — the frogs stopped their songs, and the insects froze.

He bit into it, sharing some with Kaia, who was very impressed. Frogs were one of the most delicious foods he knew of. They had a weird texture, but a sweet, smooth taste, and it had been a while since he'd eaten one.

They lay there for a while in silence. After a long while, the frogs and insects started singing again. Smiling, Kaia began stalking the sounds. Lily pads extended from the edge of the pond to the middle. The moon came into view, reflected in the still water. In that moment, everything was perfect.

A frog darted out from underneath a leaf onto one of the lily pads. Kaia pounced, following an instinct to keep it from getting away. She hovered in the air for a moment, arched gracefully. Then, with a splash, she fell below the surface of the water. Her head immediately popped up, spluttering, and she scrambled out of the pond, yelping with surprise. Water dripped from her fur, weighing it down close to her skinny body. A lily pad hung awkwardly from one of her ears. Scruff tried his best, but couldn't hide his amusement.

"Stop laughing." She glared at him.

"I'm sorry! It's just … the lily pad …" He had to sit down to steady himself.

Kaia tossed her head to dislodge the lily pad, but eventually she began to smile. "Okay, I guess it was a little funny."

"I didn't know you hated water so much."

She gave a big shake and delicately licked her paws. "Well, this proves it. Hunting is not for me. Let's head back. We can find food in the alleys on the way." Her tone was decisive.

Scruff sighed, the perfect moment gone. He helped her gently lick the pond scum off the sides of her face. It was clear he wasn't going to make any more headway in getting her to like hunting tonight. At least they could spend time together. They found plenty of bugs and garbage to eat as they headed back slowly.

It was dawn when they got back to the park. The increased human activity these days made Scruff nervous, so he was happy to crawl into the deep thicket of bushes and curl up next to Kaia. When the others joined them, Scruff was delighted to share the story of Kaia's swimming adventure. Casper seemed a bit distant, though. Scruff wondered if that was because Kaia was resting her muzzle on his back instead of Casper's.

As the sun rose, the sounds of the city lulled them all to sleep. Scruff woke when Kaia's head lifted off his back. He peered out from the bushes and saw a few large humans with weird-looking sticks. They were yelling loudly and hitting some of the bushes. It was strange behaviour. Scruff and Kaia looked at each other, equally puzzled. Scruff couldn't see the others, but he knew they were close by.

"Do you think they have food for us?" Kaia asked him.

Scruff just stared at her. It seemed very unlikely. Kaia rose and leaned forward to get a better look. "Careful!" Scruff woofed softly. The humans froze and looked in their direction.

Kaia turned back and gently nosed him. "Don't worry so much. I'm just going to see if they have any food." She took a few tentative steps toward the edge of the bushes and poked her head out. The humans immediately started making friendly noises. Kaia laughed and took a few more steps toward them. "Do you smell it?"

Then Scruff did smell it: delicious, salty meat. It wasn't rodent, but it did smell incredible. His mouth watered. Kaia put on her best show, wagging her tail gently as she carefully approached them.

Scruff lost sight of her through the leaves. Then, all of a sudden, there was a deafening bang. A wall of air burst through his ears, and an icy chill ran through him. Holding his breath, he shifted to look out through the bushes. Kaia lay slumped on the ground, gasping in pain. There was another boom. Her body jumped, then went completely still. For a moment, nothing moved or made a sound.

Then, Casper ran out from behind a different bush, barking loudly. One of the humans raised the stick in his hand, and there was another explosion. Casper fell to the ground. He took a few moaning breaths, and two more bangs rocked his body. Casper no longer moved.

In a panic, Scruff crawled backward through the thick branches, scraping the ground with his belly. On the far side of the bushes, he turned and raced away down the road. He saw nothing but the ground in front of his paws.

EIGHTEEN
GRIEF

Scruff

Only when he began gasping for air, pain rippling through his lungs, did Scruff slow down. He became aware of a bustling world around him. He was in the middle of a sidewalk, with cars honking, people not far away. The sight of humans reactivated the panic, and he careened into an alley, looking for somewhere to hide. A few blocks away, he found a thick, overgrown hedge that ran between the alley and a house. He dove into it, relief pouring through his body now that he was hidden from the world.

As his breathing slowed, his mind sped up. What had the humans done to Casper and Kaia? And what could he do? He wanted to return and help them, but fiery terror at the thought of leaving the hedge held him back. Now he knew the power of humans, and he never wanted to be near one again.

The day passed in a daze. He kept shifting positions, feeling that he needed to go back to the park to help. But, surrounded by the constant din of human noise, he couldn't bring himself to leave the safety of the bushes. As soon as night fell, the heartbeat of the Wild Lands slowed. He cautiously slid out into the alley, hugging the shadows. Every time a car passed, he cowered, shivering. Every time he heard a human, he dove for the nearest cover, unable to breathe.

When he finally made it to the park, it was almost dark. He sensed instantly that it was empty, but remained wary, sliding slowly back into the bush from where he had watched everything before. He peered out. Nothing. Kaia and Casper were gone.

He was about to leave the bush when he heard the jingling of a dog collar. A lone dog walker entered the park with a large black dog. The dog looked in Scruff's direction and began to bark, straining against his leash. Scruff backed away, cowering, but the human pulled on the leash and dragged the dog right past Scruff's hiding place.

It was a long time before he found the courage to leave the bushes. By then the night was velvety dark, and other than the occasional car, all the humans were in bed. He slunk forward, looking for the spot where Kaia had fallen. A few steps away, he smelled it: blood. The distinctive metallic odour was spread across the grass. He had smelled it many times before —occasionally when play fighting got out of hand, a few times when Jagger was hurt — but the smell had never been this strong. His stomach heaved, and he backed away. He'd finally learned the source of the humans' power. But being right about them didn't make him feel anything besides sick. His new family was gone, and his home was no longer safe.

Scruff had felt grief before. He had been alone before. But this time, it was worse. A grey cloud of guilt and terror hung over him, making it hard to think. If he had only tried a little harder, he might have been able to save Kaia. Instead, he'd relaxed his guard, and now Kaia and Casper were dead.

And Pica. He felt even sicker when he thought about her. She'd been right all along. She had always stood up for what she believed was true, even if it meant hurting his feelings. She had been right to be so mad at him for taking that bread, and he'd pushed her away. And now she was gone. They were all gone.

Lying under the hedge, unsure of what to do, he found himself replaying the past over and over again. A day passed, and eventually he rose to get some water, following his instincts and not really noticing where he was going. After finding a puddle, he returned to the hedge. The next day, he did the same.

A few times, he thought about going back to the park to see if Noodle and Chica were there. But everything about the park repelled him now, and even if he did find them, what would he say? Kaia had been their North Star, and without her, there was nothing to give them a shared direction.

As time passed, he was gradually able to venture out into the world beyond the hedge again. Although his mind was numb, something deep in his body compelled him to go out each night to find food and water. He waited until the night was a deep, dark black and stuck to the train tracks or the scrubby beaches along the water, avoiding the busy roads and the houses farther up the hill. These days, even a passing car made his heart beat faster. He became a transient shadow, each night finding just enough food to survive before locating a new safe spot to hide out for the day. Each day felt longer than the last.

One night, he was heading out from his latest hideout to the train tracks, hungry for a meal, when he sensed something that electrified his whole body. He stepped toward a long concrete wall at the edge of a parking lot and froze, blending in as best he could. He scanned the parking lot and the low building nearby. A cool breeze blew a plastic bag up into the air, and a few dark cars hulked silently in the darkness. Nothing seemed out of place. Then, at the far side of the parking lot, a shape glided around the building, heading in his direction. He knew that shape. Jagger.

Scruff cursed his carelessness. It was not too far from the ravine where he had smelled Jagger before. He should have avoided this area completely, ducking into the neighbourhoods to avoid a possible confrontation. This was the last thing Scruff needed. The shape glided into the middle of the parking lot and then froze. Jagger turned his head to stare straight at Scruff.

"Scruff?"

"Jagger." Scruff would not be cowed this time. He stepped out from the wall and walked with his head high over to where Jagger stood. His muscles were tense, waiting for an aggressive sign from Jagger, but his tail was low, his ears relaxed. "It's a surprise to find you here," he ventured.

"I could say the same."

They stared at each other for a few moments. The last time Scruff had seen Jagger was on the golf course with Pica, right when they'd found out that it had been taken over by humans to build their houses on. Jagger had been there, and when Scruff had demanded to know whether Jagger had killed their parents, Jagger's response was cryptic: "You runts really have no idea. No idea at all." He'd laughed and then just walked off. Scruff had never seen him again. Until now.

Jagger broke the silence. "Are you living over here with Pica now?"

Scruff swallowed awkwardly, a huge lump in his throat. "No, I live here on my own."

"What happened to her?"

He wasn't about to get into it. "It didn't work out."

Jagger laughed deeply at this. "This isn't an easy place to make a life, is it?"

"No."

"You starting to learn more about life?"

"What do you mean?" Scruff tried to read Jagger's expression.

"You always fought me about everything. Working to get a better territory, keeping away from other packs, making sure we looked out for ourselves first. Basic coyote things. You always wanted everyone to get along, or something. I wonder if you see now that it's hard everywhere. You have to fight for what you want."

"I'm doing fine here."

Jagger cocked his head to the side. "I don't believe you. But that doesn't matter. You never cared what I thought, anyway." He paused and then turned back. "Nice to run into you. Anytime you want to talk, you know where to find me."

With that, he glided away through the parking lot and into the darkness.

NINETEEN
SENTINEL

Pica

Just before dawn the next day, Pica went around to each member of the pack and said goodbye. She touched her nose to theirs gently, sniffed them, and invited them to do a group howl. Warmth hadn't yet spread to the landscape as they stood, waiting. Leila began with a single note. Then a few more coyotes joined in. Pica added notes of sadness and longing. The tones wound around each other, becoming a single song that filled Pica's heart. When they finished, there was nothing more that needed to be said. She flicked her ears at Rooney and headed off.

"Are you still sure about this?" she said over her shoulder.

"Stop worrying, Pica. It's only a day to the mountains. Let's just get it done."

This time, the trip across the plains toward the distant mountains felt less scary. Having Rooney at her side made a big difference, and the landscape was no longer foreign to her. Now she knew what the smells were and could pick the best routes around the large farms and ranches that dotted the land. They kept the road within earshot, crossing it once to avoid a large farm, but generally they stayed in the fields. Pica was alert for any sign of wolves or any weird smells that might indicate a trap. She would not get stuck again.

She was slightly slower than Rooney and had to rest periodically when her bad leg cramped up from being used so much. Her good front leg was sore and tired, but it wasn't too bad. She felt excited seeing the mountains draw closer throughout the day. They rose up high, blocking the sky in front of her. Eventually, she could see definition on each mountain: white on top, with lots of jagged rocks and scraggly trees clinging to the sides. They were beautiful, but as they loomed larger, she began to wonder whether she was strong enough to get over them.

A few times, they heard wolves howling, but they were far enough away that they didn't have to change course. The sun shone down on them, warm but not too hot. The wind was light, and it felt nice ruffling her thick coat. They were making good progress.

By the time the sun slid behind the mountains, they had reached a series of low hills. The road began to wind, so they took a straight path to cut off unnecessary distance. They trotted gently across the uneven earth, and Pica noticed that when she was in the dips between hills, she couldn't see the mountains. This was disorienting, since she was using the mountains as a reference point. She made a mental note to pay attention and relocate the road each time she emerged from a dip.

"We should probably find some more food and get some rest," Rooney said.

"Yes, but I want to go as far as I can today," Pica replied. Now that she had started her trip, she felt a driving need to keep going. Also, in the back of her mind, she was acutely aware that tomorrow morning, she would be on her own.

She did feel hungry, though, so they slowed down. Along the flank of the next hill, they entered a meadow filled with low bushes and long, soft grass. They stepped gently and crouched low, ears swivelling. Pica heard a telltale scraping sound to her right and froze, head cocked. She could feel the vibration with her paws, and her eyes confirmed that it was a small snake. Without taking a breath, she pounced. Leaping up effortlessly, she dropped both front paws — the injured one and the non-injured — down onto the snake. The claws of her good paw clamped into it, and before it could get away, she reached down and bit it, shaking it firmly.

"That was awesome!" Rooney yipped. "That was like you had all four paws back."

Pica dropped the lifeless snake in front of her. "Snakes are easier than ground squirrels."

"That doesn't matter. As long as you catch something from time to time, plus all the grass and bugs to eat, you'll get by, no problem."

She craned her head up to look at the mountain in front of her. It was hard to tell how many snakes might be living up there. But she figured she might as well enjoy the current moment — and the snack — and leave the worry for tomorrow morning.

They headed onward for another hour, keeping an ear out for food. Pica didn't catch anything else, but she did help scare a few things in Rooney's direction.

It grew cold, then dark. They found a hollow underneath an old, dead tree that smelled like it had been used by some kind of weasel, though no one had been there recently. There was just enough space for both of them to curl up. Pica suppressed a sigh as she lay down. It was a relief to rest her legs. Today had been the farthest she had travelled in a day since her injury; she was definitely going to feel it tomorrow.

Despite the knowledge that she was leaving Rooney and the pack, she'd had a wonderful day. There were dangers out here, but trotting along in the big, beautiful fields with Rooney, the rhythm of their paws making a kind of music, was almost meditative. She wanted to stay up and soak it all in, but the warm body next to her and the sound of slow, even breathing soon lulled her to sleep.

She woke every now and then to sniff the air or turn to her other side. A large, full moon shone down on them, casting shadows into the hollow. At times she could tell that Rooney was awake, too, by the changes in his breathing.

They didn't talk, though. Both waited in their warm co-coon for the sun to illuminate the world around them.

It started with a glow. With their backs to the mountains, they were facing the direction where Rooney's family was. Pica saw a bright spot rise up over the horizon and wondered what the rest of the pack was doing right now. Were they also watching the sunrise? Were they wondering whether Rooney would make it back safely? She felt him shift and lay his head gently on her neck. It was a bold move that normally would have made her feel very uncomfortable. But she could sense he was getting ready to say goodbye, and this was his way of telling her how much he would miss her.

She turned her head and gently licked the side of his face. "I'll miss you a lot, you know."

He ducked his head. "I'll miss you a lot, too."

There was so much more she wanted to say. That she was incredibly grateful to him for taking care of her. That she loved his pack and this landscape. That a big part of her wanted to stay, but it just didn't feel right. In the end, she simply crawled out of the tree well, had a deep stretch, and said, "Be careful getting back today — no investigating weird smells. Straight back through until you're safe."

Rooney slid out beside her and gave her a gentle bump on the hip. "Yes, Mom."

"You know what I mean."

"It's you who needs to be careful. Travel fast, and be smart. Find some more snakes! You just need to go up and over these mountains and then you'll be in the Wild Lands. I know you can do it."

Pica leaned into him. "Say thank you to Leila for helping me. I would have died in that trap without her."

"I will."

"Okay."

"Okay."

She stood there, not knowing how to take the next step. Finally, Rooney sighed.

"Well, you'd better get going. You have mountains to climb. Remember to sleep low in the night; it will be warmer. And cross the ice carefully. And drink all the water you can whenever you see it."

"Yes, Mom."

"Not fair."

"You started it."

Pica was going to miss this. She didn't want to be on her own.

Rooney gave a final stretch and shook out his fur. He looked straight into her eyes with determination and strength. "Best of luck, Pica. I'll be thinking about you." And with a final wag of his tail, he turned and headed back toward his home.

Pica stood there and watched him go. She fought the urge to call out, ask for one more hour with him. Looking back over her shoulder, she shuddered. The mountain rose up above her, a tall, unknowable sentinel. This was new terrain, and she had to face it alone.

PART FIVE

NEW LEAVES

TWENTY
RAVINE

Scruff

After Scruff's run-in with Jagger, the rest of the night was a blur. He picked his way uphill, thoughts of hunting abandoned. He didn't care where he ended up — he just needed to gain some distance from Jagger and the ugly memories of the past that were resurfacing. After an hour or so, feeling more comfortable, he came across a small green space behind a store that hadn't been claimed by another coyote, and he curled up out of sight.

Memories bounced around his head. Jagger feeding him when he was barely old enough to hunt. Long, lonely days watching Pica's family play in the field, wondering where Jagger was and why he didn't play with Scruff in the same way. Meeting Pica for the first time, and Jagger's rage when he found out that Scruff had befriended the rival pack next door. Machines destroying their forest home, building more houses for humans. Jagger attacking Pica's family in order to drive them away and secure the beautiful golf course for himself. And for Scruff.

That was the hard part. In everything that Jagger had done, he'd always protected Scruff. Even when that meant destroying the pack next door by killing their alpha male and running them off their land. Scruff could never forgive him for that, but he was starting to understand Jagger's toughness and desperation. Life was hard in the Wild Lands, and it hammered home the point that Jagger had always made: you have to fight hard for a good place to live.

Ever since Pica had told him that Jagger was actually Scruff's older brother from a previous litter and that he had saved Scruff after his parents died, he had been torn. Jagger had tricked him into helping to kill Pica's father, thus ruining her family. For that, he felt seething hatred for Jagger. But at the same time, he was grateful that Jagger had rescued him as a pup — he would otherwise have died long ago. The one question that kept rising above all the others was whether Jagger had really cared about him or had just been using Scruff to further his own purposes. If he had run Pica's family off the land, would he still have welcomed Scruff as a brother? Scruff had never figured that out.

He had buried these emotions and questions for a long time, but as the day passed and darkness fell, they throbbed in his brain. Maybe they felt more important now that everyone else in Scruff's life was gone, and Jagger was the last connection to his old life. He wanted to understand what had motivated Jagger to care for him back then and to find out how he felt now.

As soon as it was completely dark, Scruff began to hunt for the ravine where Jagger lived. He couldn't remember exactly where it was, so it took him hours of searching. Finally, he recognized his surroundings and followed Jagger's scent paths to the edge of the deep chasm. Old houses lined the edge of the ravine, their backyard fences crumbling down the steep slope. He easily found a way through one of the fences, and half walked, half-slid down the slope to the cold, thin creek at the bottom. Once there, he looked around cautiously. Jagger's smell was everywhere, though he wasn't here at the moment.

Scruff lay down to wait, at first too tense to enjoy the calm gurgling of the creek. Eventually, though, the peacefulness of the setting began to relax him. It was a good spot, very private and safe.

A few hours later, he heard footsteps, and his shoulder muscles tensed. Jagger's tall form slipped down the bank and joined him at the bottom of the ravine. Scruff stood.

Jagger's eyes slid over to him, showing no surprise. He paused to drink deeply before approaching. "Welcome."

"Hi, Jagger." There was a long silence. "So ..." Scruff began, his throat feeling tight. "How did you end up over here in the Wild Lands?" There was so much more he wanted to ask, but he didn't know how to begin.

"Looking for a place to stay, same as you, I imagine."

Silence again. Jagger's tone wasn't unfriendly, but he wasn't making this easy, either. Scruff was going to have to keep pushing. "I know you're my brother," he barked. "Pica told me. Why did you hide that from me?"

"I didn't hide it from you."

"You never told me. Or why you adopted me. I never knew that …" He trailed off, not sure what he actually wanted to say.

"I don't like talking about it."

"Well, I don't like being kept in the dark. I never knew anything about my family, and all you did was lie to me." Scruff felt the fur on his shoulders rise, revealing his anger and frustration.

"You could never just be content. You shouldn't have needed an explanation. You just needed to see the reality in front of you. We had a pack, and we had a beautiful forest, but you spent every minute daydreaming about Pica's family." Jagger laughed. "It looks like following your heart worked out pretty well for you."

That sarcastic, biting tone made Scruff felt like a pup all over again, cowed by his bigger, fiercer pack mate. Why had he thought that coming here was a good idea? Jagger was just a bully. Brother or not, Scruff would rather be on his own. He stood up and started to leave without a backward glance. But before he got halfway up the bank, he heard Jagger's voice again.

"Scruff, stop. I'll tell you."

He whipped his head around. He'd never heard this pleading tone before and didn't know whether to trust it. He paused with his feet pointing uphill and his head looking back, unsure of his next move.

Jagger beckoned him. "I'll tell you about our parents."

Scruff turned around. He would do anything to hear more about his parents.

Jagger began talking, the words spilling out. Scruff lay down and listened with surprise as Jagger told him he'd grown up in a litter of nine. Scruff had never heard of a litter that size before.

"I was one of the stronger ones. Three of the others didn't even survive the first few weeks. Mom and Dad tried to find enough food, but with so many, we were always hungry." His voice became low and bitter. "I tried my best to help, but they always liked my sisters best. One day, I fought with one of my sisters over a mouse, or something dumb like that. She ran to Mom and complained, and right then and there, with no warning, Mom told me to get out." Jagger stopped.

Scruff broke the long pause. "What do you mean, get out?"

"There wasn't enough food or space for all of us. And we were getting old enough to make a go of it. So she just chased me off, told me not to come back."

Scruff watched the emotions come and go on Jagger's face as he filled in the rest of his childhood: wandering around on his own through that first winter, almost dying of hunger, but somehow making it through. He'd tried to find a home territory, but there wasn't much out there, and he wasn't big enough to defend it, anyway.

"Eventually, something drew me back home. Not love for my family exactly, but a strong pull. I don't know. I'd always thought about them and wondered how they were. But when I finally went back, everyone was gone — well, everyone but you. I smelled birth and death, but the only living thing was you, a tiny, scrawny thing trying to fight off a crow. Your littermates were dead, and there was no sign of our parents."

Scruff sat up. He remembered that day well.

"I laughed at you, trying to chase off that bird. I hadn't laughed like that in a long time. I figured the forest was mine now, and I really didn't feel like killing you. So I let you live with me. But, as you grew, you irritated me more and more. You look exactly like Dad, and you sound like him, too. Sometimes it brought me back to those days when I was never good enough. I'd take off and leave you for a while. And you spent all of your time mooning over that golf course family. It was clear which pack you wanted to be a part of."

"But ..." Scruff started to protest, but it was true. He had always wished he was in Pica's family.

"And when the forest was destroyed for that housing development and I wanted to take over the golf course territory, you were so stubborn. You ruined everything. You had no idea how hard it would be to find a new territory, what it was like to have no home. If you'd followed my plan, we'd be fat and happy now."

Scruff frowned. "That's not true! The golf course is gone now, too. I was there, remember? That was the last time I saw you."

"Of course I remember," Jagger said, his voice bitter again. "No, it's not a golf course anymore, but there's still good land nearby. We could have pushed out another coyote and made a home somewhere near there. But you were blind." The familiar mocking tone returned. "What happened to her, again?"

"Pica?"

"Who else?"

Scruff hesitated. It was all too raw. Although the older coyote had finally shared his story, Scruff wasn't yet ready to let Jagger into the deepest areas of his heart. He repeated what he'd already told Jagger, hoping it would again be enough and they could move on. "Uh, it didn't work out. We decided to go our own ways. I don't know where she is now."

They were both silent for a moment, thinking. Scruff finally understood why Jagger had adopted him and why he was so bitter all the time. "Thank you."

"For what?"

"For finally telling me everything. And for saving me when I was a pup." He left it at that, not wanting to get into it any deeper.

But something still nagged at him. Even if rescuing him had been Jagger's way of making a home and a family, hadn't Jagger been mean to him and driven him away? Scruff couldn't be sure anymore what was real and what he had simply interpreted incorrectly. The only thing he did know was that now, Jagger was his only family in the world.

Jagger nodded at him. "You're looking rough. You can use this as a home base for now, if you want. I don't mind."

Scruff's body felt heavy all of a sudden after such an emotional conversation. He let out a big yawn and lay down. "Thanks." Closing his eyes, he felt safe for the first time in weeks.

TWENTY-ONE
HUNTED

Pica

The first hour had been the hardest. Climbing higher and higher, Pica left everything familiar behind. As she lost sight of the foothills, it felt like the mountains were swallowing her up. Remembering how disorienting it could be between the hills, she made sure to keep the big road in sight. Her muscles ached, but she ignored them, pushing steadily uphill toward the first pass.

The landscape changed gradually. It became rockier, and there were different kinds of trees. She recognized a few of the plants from parks in the Wild Lands, but there were many that she'd never seen before. Around midday, she reached a beautiful crystal-clear lake surrounded by large boulders on all sides and drank with relief. The water was so cold that it burned her throat going down. She looked around for possible danger. Despite the peaceful feeling, she didn't trust this new landscape.

She heard a loud squeak from above and looked up to see the largest, fattest rodent she'd ever seen sitting up on one of the rocks, staring at her. Her mouth started to water. That was one delicious-looking meal. She took a few steps toward it. It didn't move, but it squeaked again. Then came another squeak, this time from close behind her. She whirled to see another one of the rodents. Sizing them up, she was pretty sure she could kill one. They were probably slow moving.

She bounded toward the closest one. A split-second later, it dove down into a hole between two boulders. She tried to stick her head down the hole to grab it, but it was long gone. She couldn't even hear it anymore. Then, it popped out of a different hole a ways to her left, squeaking and squealing away. It was laughing at her. She huffed, surprised.

Unable to resist the temptation, again she leapt at it. This time, she caught her good leg between some rocks and got mocked again, this time by three rodents. Sighing in frustration, she admitted defeat and gave up. For the next hour, as she slowly picked her way upward between the big boulders, she endured mockery by dozens of the fat little things, each one sitting just a few feet away. She was so hungry it took all of her resolve not to waste her energy on them.

She neared the top of the ridge and picked up her pace, eager to find out whether she'd be able to see the Wild Lands or the city on the other side. A few more big rocks, and then she was there! She eagerly looked around … and her whole body grew heavy as she processed what she saw. She was not at the top of the mountain at all, but only part of the way up. A line of ridges loomed far above her, casting large shadows over the valleys. The road wound up the side of one of them before diving over a saddle. Everything was so much larger than it had looked from below.

She flopped down with a sigh to munch on some grass and give her legs a rest. Suddenly, she caught a faint scent — a musty, salty odour that was very familiar, though she couldn't quite place it. Then, it clicked. Images of large, glowing eyes and paws the size of her head cascaded into her mind's eye. A monster cat lived here. The scent wasn't fresh, but she was risking great danger by staying in one place. She had to press on.

Her muscles complained as she stood up again. Hearing a small rustle behind her, she whipped her head around and nervously scanned the area. Just the wind. Swivelling her ears back and forth, she quickly descended the other side of the ridge toward the small valley. Thankfully, going down was easier than going up, and she didn't smell or hear any more sign of the big cat. Shivering, she did smell some wolf scat, but it wasn't fresh. She reached the bottom of the valley and headed up a ridgeline that led to the big peak, travelling in parallel to the road. A line of cars and trucks zipped along the highway, cresting the mountain, then disappearing. They were so powerful. Her journey here in that truck had been so much easier and faster than this journey on foot.

She could see the ice now — she was getting close. She marvelled at the beauty of it, but her body was beginning to drag with exhaustion. She lost awareness of her surroundings, focusing only on where to plant her next step. Her muscles began to cramp from exhaustion and from holding up her bad leg. There was still plenty of light, but she wouldn't be able to go much farther tonight.

With her next step, her paw crunched into cold, icy white stuff. She looked up — she had reached the snow! Just up ahead, the road dipped out of sight. After that, she'd be going downhill again. She just needed to get past this snow and down the next hill, and then she would be able to stop and rest. Tentatively, she took another step. The snow was firm, and her claws dug in. Good. The coolness gave her paws some relief.

This relief was short lived, however, as she realized that ice was more difficult than dirt to travel on. Although her claws dug in, the top layer was hard, and sometimes her paws slipped, making her fall over. With only three good legs, she felt like a day-old pup all over again.

After struggling for a while, she glanced up and noticed that the sun had fallen behind the peak. How much time was left until it got fully dark? She glanced longingly at the road, which had neither snow nor ice. Unfortunately, it was far too full of cars for her to use. She had to press on.

A bitter wind kicked up. It was so much colder up here. She hesitated, wondering if she should retreat to the valley for the night. But her body rebelled at the idea of turning around. She had spent so much effort in getting here that she had to keep going.

Carefully, she picked her way onward. Just as dusk fell, she reached the saddle — the highest point before her descent — and felt nothing but awe for a moment. A soft-pink sunset bathed the sky, and everywhere she looked, pointed white peaks reached up. She had never seen anything like this. The ache in her muscles faded away.

Tracking the course of the road, she felt a vague uneasiness about how it curved around the next mountain and disappeared into the distance. How many more mountains would she have to cross to get back to the city? She didn't let herself dwell on that thought too long, though. She had to hurry. She wanted to be back on dirt again before it got fully dark. Already the sky was starting to darken, pink fading to purple.

But unlike travelling on dirt, descending on ice was much harder than going up it. The crusty layer that had given her claws some purchase on the ascent didn't offer any grip now that she was going down. She picked her way along a narrow ridge, her legs shaking, and made sure to breathe slowly as she placed each foot down. She focused all of her concentration on not slipping. Suddenly, a raven swooped over her head, calling out a warning. Her heart began to thud — ravens were rarely wrong. She stopped and turned her head from side to side, searching. On the stiff, cold breeze, she caught the scent of the monster cat.

Abandoning all caution, she slipped and slid down the slope. She steadied herself and took a big leap across a hole in the ice, but her good front paw landed awkwardly, and she stumbled. This time, none of her paws could get a grip. Yelping and twisting, she tried to set her claws into the ice, but she was sliding too fast now. All her worries about the cat disappeared as the world became a blur, and suddenly, she couldn't feel the ground anymore. Her body began to tumble. A shriek erupted from her as her legs pinwheeled through open air. Then, her body hit something hard. Up was down and down was up as she tumbled some more, bouncing off jagged surfaces, getting the air knocked out of her. At last, with a final lurch, she came to a stop.

She tried to lift her head, but the world was spinning. Pain washed through her body. She lowered her head back down and lay there, trying to catch her breath. She hoped the big cat hadn't followed her. Disoriented as she was, there was no way she'd be able to run away.

After a few minutes, she managed to lift her throbbing head and look around. She had come to rest in a damp clump of grass at the edge of a large meadow. Above her rose a steep cliff, chunks of ice clinging to the rock. In the advancing darkness, she could make out some trees on the other side of the meadow.

She stood gingerly. Although she ached in a thousand places, her legs still worked, and she didn't seem to have any deep gashes, just a few scrapes and bruises and a very sore head. She walked a bit, testing herself. One of her back legs hurt where a rock had bashed her knee, but she exhaled in relief, realizing she was in surprisingly good shape, considering the fall. Even so, she wasn't going any farther tonight. She crossed the meadow and sniffed around carefully in the trees before deciding that it was safe enough. She didn't have much choice. She found a depression in the ground under a tree and curled up in it, her head throbbing a steady beat until she fell asleep.

TWENTY-TWO
BROTHERS

Scruff

Scruff woke to cold, hard river rocks pushing into his ribs. Feeling the deep-seated exhaustion of his body and his mind, he groaned, not wanting to face the day. Then, he sniffed. There was something wonderful here. He cracked open an eye to see some meat lying in front of him. Rabbit. He quickly raised his head and looked around, remembering where he was, but didn't see Jagger anywhere.

Scruff dug in enthusiastically. Energy flooded into him as he chewed. He finished and sat up, feeling better. The sun was up, though it didn't filter all the way down the ravine. Bright-green maple leaves, newly unfurled, provided shade. The only sounds were the quiet splashes and bubbles of the creek.

He stretched and sniffed the air. Where had Jagger gone? He was surprised to realize that he was looking forward to seeing Jagger again. If nothing else, he was a familiar face. His brother.

Brother. It sounded weird to say. With his wiry body covered in scars, Jagger had always seemed much older than just a few litters before Scruff. Hearing how he'd been cast out from the family at such a young age and forced to fend for himself, Scruff had felt sympathy. It also explained why Jagger had pushed Scruff so hard to become independent.

Scruff weighed his options. Pica was gone, Kaia was dead, and he didn't want to be alone anymore. At least for now, it would be nice to establish a home base and have someone looking out for him. He didn't anticipate forming a strong bond with Jagger and didn't entirely trust him, but knowing he was here helped push away the dark, empty feeling that had threatened to envelop Scruff.

Jagger returned a few hours later, his slim, dark body winding gracefully between the bushes on the banks of the creek. Scruff stood tall and greeted him with a tail wag. Warm, though a bit aloof. This was the tone he would try to set from here on in.

"Thanks for the rabbit."

"No problem. How are you feeling?"

"Good." There was an awkward silence. "I think I will stay here awhile, at least until I get back my strength. If it's okay with you."

"Whatever you need. It would be helpful to have another coyote here in case anyone challenges me."

"All right. Thanks."

Jagger briefly rested his head on top of Scruff's neck, and Scruff allowed it, feeling the weight and the dominance the gesture conveyed. Then Jagger released him and moved away.

Scuff peered up through the tree canopy, shaking out his fur. "I'm cold. I'm going to do a quick hunt before it gets too late in the morning. See you soon." He quickly turned and left, purposely not waiting for Jagger's assent. This was a new relationship dynamic. He was old enough to take care of himself now. Living with Jagger was his choice, not his only option for survival. He'd give it a few weeks and see how it felt.

As the weeks passed, Scruff was surprised by how smoothly things were going. It was nice to know that, at the end of every night, he had a safe, quiet place to curl up for the day. He slept more deeply knowing that Jagger was there. As time passed, his crippling fear of humans waned until he was able to hunt near roads and houses again.

Conversations with Jagger were short, and Scruff still felt lonely, but this situation was much better than any alternative he could think of, so he settled into the rhythm. He explored different areas of the city, familiarizing himself with the coyotes who lived there and their territories. He always kept an eye out for a good potential territory and for Pica's scent. He wasn't going to take anything for granted. Mostly, he spent lots of time relaxing in the ravine, slightly bored as he waited to go hunting or to see Jagger.

Although he was still very fearful of humans, he spent a lot of time watching them, trying to understand them better. There was a park not far from the ravine that was so busy with human activity that no coyote had claimed it for a territory. Once, Scruff decided to spend the day there, tucked into the shelter offered by a clump of bushes in the far corner. Some humans kicked a ball around, yelling loudly. There was a playground where water sprayed in the afternoons, and the smaller humans ran through the water, shrieking with joy and sometimes crying.

Good food smells made Scruff's mouth water. He worked each nostril carefully, learning everything he could about the food. It reminded him of Kaia, and as soon as it was dusk, he returned to the ravine, feeling sadder than he'd been in weeks.

One afternoon, when the heat was at its highest, Scruff and Jagger were both relaxing in the ravine. It had proven to be a perfect summer spot, because even though the stream had dwindled to a trickle, they could still wet their paws in it and drink the water. Scruff had just stretched and curled up again when he smelled new coyotes. He stood and gave a short bark. Jagger jumped up, too. They stood side by side, a team.

There were two intruders, both greyish in colour. The female was small but looked strong. The male was sick and had lost much of his fur. They stopped and assessed Jagger and Scruff, their ears alert.

A low, deep growl started in Jagger's throat. Scruff growled, too. "Move on," he said, surprising himself.

The other coyotes considered for a second. Then, the female caught the male's eye and communicated a silent no. They turned on their heels and trotted away.

Scruff took a deep breath. Success! He felt good and turned to Jagger to share in the victory, but instead, Jagger reproachfully snapped his teeth in Scruff's direction.

"Next time, let me do the talking. I'm bigger."

Heat spread through Scruff's body. What was Jagger's problem? Scruff was strong, practically an adult now. He knew better than to challenge Jagger, though. Scruff lowered his tail and bowed his head in apology. Jagger snuffled, then methodically started to re-mark their boundary. Scruff followed, adding his own scent, and then they lay back down. He reminded himself that he had chosen to stay, knowing full well that Jagger would be the dominant member of the pack. At least they had successfully defended their territory.

Later that night, when the temperature had dropped and darkness had fallen, he went out. Jagger didn't even raise his head. Scruff climbed the ravine and wound his way slowly to the park where the water sprayed. Sniffing around, he tracked the events of the day through the smells coating the earth. He sat down on the cool and damp cement in the middle of the water-spraying area and looked up. The stars were dimly visible, dotting the sky. A low, mournful howl escaped him. It soothed him, so he continued, calling out his grief. He said goodbye to Pica and goodbye to Kaia. He said goodbye to the playful side of himself that had dreamed of laughing through each day. He mourned all of his losses, and with a final, trembling note, accepted that they were gone. He was now a mostly solitary coyote sharing a territory with Jagger. He had food, strength, and basic companionship. He had a safe place to sleep at night. No longer would he dream of having anything more. Surviving in this world was difficult, and he should be proud that he had gotten to the point of being able to take care of himself. This was his life now, and he was ready to live it.

TWENTY-THREE
PICNIC

Pica

The morning after her fall, Pica had awoken exhausted and hungry. Scared to move, she had lifted her head slowly, feeling the throbbing pain return. Her body felt like lead. She was one big bruise.

Sighing, she had gotten up and resumed her journey, now keeping the road close as the ground flattened out into open grassland. She had found a patch of early berries and picked them greedily off the bush. The tart juice running down her parched throat had given her a burst of energy. However, the black, snaking pavement of the road winding up another mountain reminded her just how far she had to go.

The next few days were rough, an unending series of painful steps. She crested ridges and descended them. She found snakes, berries, and bugs, yet still, she felt a little weaker every day. Luckily, there was water everywhere, and gulping cold mouthfuls of creek water gave her some energy. The only thing that kept her going was thinking of Scruff and telling herself that the Wild Lands would be just on the other side of the next ridge. But this strategy made her depressed each time she reached the top of a ridge to face yet more mountains.

This evening, as the light began to turn the mountain peaks pink, Pica trotted along slowly, her feet swollen, the skin of her paw pads almost worn away. Her mind wandered in and out, and she kept stumbling. Her whole body screamed at her to stop and lie down. She was considering it when she heard a distant wolf howl. Her spirits sank. She couldn't stay here tonight.

She was almost at the top of a small ridge, and she pushed herself to reach it. Maybe there would be something on the other side. Her paws scrabbling across large boulders, she finally reached the peak and looked down, not daring to hope for much. She blinked twice, then yelped with surprise. There *was* something there! At the bottom of the valley, the big road led straight to a large cluster of houses, buildings, and smaller roads. It was not the city or the Wild Lands, but it was the closest thing she'd seen since she left. She picked up speed, angling straight toward the town.

Pulling into the outskirts, she saw her first familiar sight: a Dumpster. Relief flooded into her. It was all so familiar — the smell of human food wafting from the houses and some of the buildings, the oily odour of gasoline, and the hum of the wires that stretched overhead. Finding a space between the Dumpster and the wall of a building, she collapsed. Here, she could rest for the night. Her brain and body shut down, too exhausted to even plan the next day.

The next morning, a loud beeping sound woke her. Her brain was foggy, and her tongue was swollen in her mouth. She had only enough energy to lift her head and see a truck backing up to the building, right next to the Dumpster. She blinked. It looked so similar to the one she had been trapped inside what seemed like years ago. Sniffing the air gently, she sighed. Different, though. There was no sweet smell coming from this one. Just a musty chemical smell.

As she was waited for the humans to go inside the building, she realized that she might be stuck here for the day. She'd gotten so used to travelling by day and sleeping at night that she'd forgotten the rhythm of the humans. She wouldn't be able to travel through a strange town and find food in broad daylight. But she couldn't go on without food. Sighing, she dropped her heavy head back onto her paws and prepared to wait.

The day was long, but she was so exhausted that she napped through most of it. Finally, the light faded, and it was nighttime. She crept out from behind the Dumpster, groaning as her muscles seized up from having been inactive for so long. Cautiously, she began to explore the town, surprised at how unsteady she felt. She tried to remember how many days she'd gone without food, but couldn't even remember how many days she'd been travelling. Luckily, the landscape of houses, sidewalks, and alleys felt so familiar that she was mostly on autopilot. She smelled other coyote markings, but knew how to steer clear of them, and thankfully, she didn't sense any wolves or monster cats.

Unfortunately for her, the garbage bins in this town were very well secured. In the city and the Wild Lands, people left garbage in bags behind their houses or in bins whose lids fell off if she knocked against them. Here, however, the bins were tall and sturdy, and their lids didn't fall off even when she pushed them over entirely. She did find a few scraps of food in a small park and a dead squirrel under a tree, but by the time the sun started coming up, she'd covered the entire town with very little luck. Also, the small amount of food she'd eaten had woken up her stomach; every few minutes, it reminded her how hungry she was, growling at her to keep looking.

The hope that had blossomed in her when she first saw the town was gone. She had two options: stay and comb the town one more time, hoping she'd missed something, or leave to try her luck on the next mountain. Right now, though, she was too exhausted and dizzy to make a decision. She backtracked to the park and lay down under a thin bush. It wasn't a great cover, but she was too tired to look for another spot.

Night gave way to day, but she was barely aware of it. That afternoon, a group of humans came to the park and sat at a table not far from where Pica lay. She was awake, and her senses went on high alert when they opened bag after bag of delicious-smelling food. She watched, drooling, as they laid it out and proceeded to eat. She was attuned to every sound: the crinkle of the bags, the scraping of the plates, even the sound of their chewing. Eventually, one of the humans produced a ball, and they all went over to the grass to kick it around.

Pica stared at the table. There were piles of food still heaped on it. She nervously glanced at the humans. Their attention was completely focused on their game. She'd never before taken such a big risk, but if she didn't get some food now, she'd never make it back to the Wild Lands. She jumped to her feet, but quickly had to lie down again when blackness threatened to envelop her vision. Her ears rang as she tried again, more slowly this time. She took a deep breath. She had told herself she would never steal food from humans. But right now, it was a matter of life or death.

Summoning all of her strength, she broke from the bushes, raced to the table, and put her paws up on it. She heard a shout as the humans saw her, but her focus was on the picnic table. Her nose led her immediately to a large plate of meat, and she wolfed it down. She glanced up to see the humans slowly approaching the table, so she grabbed the biggest piece of food she could fit into her mouth, turned, and fled from the park. As she crossed the road, a car honked, and there was a squeal as another car slowed down, but she dodged to the side and kept going, feeling more awake and alive than she had in many days.

She dodged into an alley and galloped to the other end. Looking behind her to confirm that no humans were following her, she squeezed behind a small shed, dropped the rest of the food in front of her, and gulped it down, barely tasting it. She stood there, sides heaving, feeling the food hit her stomach. The guilt of taking such a risk melted away as she lay down in the shade behind the shed. Her stomach was beginning to digest the food, and strength was returning to her. She laid her head down on her paws, wishing she could tell Scruff what had just happened. She'd come a long way since the argument that had launched this whole nightmare. How funny that it might just be human food that would get her home.

TWENTY-FOUR

THE SEARCH

Pica

Although the meal had returned some strength to Pica's body, she still wasn't strong enough to make it over any more mountains. Emboldened by her success, the next afternoon she roamed the town looking for more easy sources of food. This time, it was a bunch of humans eating at a group of tables behind a large, low building. A bell rang, and most of them ran inside. A few humans stayed behind to clean up. Pica darted in to steal the leftovers.

She was surprised at how easy it was. The humans didn't try to chase her or attack her. They just watched or ran away. Each time, she grew a little more bold and more willing to try it again. After three days of stealing food, her belly was once again sticking out, and she felt strong enough to continue.

As morning broke, she said goodbye to the town. She was a little reluctant to swap the comfort of the town for the wilderness again, but she was also keenly aware of each day passing. She followed the road out of town, skirting the outlying houses. Soon, she was climbing upward through lush fields of grass and wildflowers. She found her stride and began what she knew would be another long day.

It turned out that having food in her belly made a huge difference. She made it to the top of the first pass before the sun had reached its peak, and she felt much steadier on the ice as she descended, now that her legs weren't shaky and weak. She was close to the top of the next pass when the sun began to lower in the sky. The last steps were dicey, as she hopped between boulders and ice. Twice, she thought she had reached the peak, but there was yet another boulder field to cross, rising higher and higher. Cold air rushed into her lungs as she panted with the effort. Her paws scrabbling against steep rock, she finally reached the top and gazed down the other side.

And there it was. The ocean. The train tracks. And way off in the distance, a haze of human development. The city and the Wild Lands. The whole time she'd been in that town, she had only been two mountains away from home! She couldn't take her eyes off the sight, and her heart threatened to beat right out of her chest. Part of her hadn't truly believed she would make it back. But here she was. She'd be there before the next day.

That night was a blur. She descended the ice carefully, then broke into a quick trot as she followed the mountain down, through rock fields and forests. The food she'd eaten in the town was still sustaining her, and she covered ground quickly.

Finally, after hours of effort, she reached a plateau that looked over the city. After taking a break to drink from a creek, she gazed down at the twinkling lights. She could not make out the ocean or the train tracks in the dark, but the smells drifting up on the night breeze were comfortingly familiar. She curled up to lick her sore paws, trying to decide whether she should keep going. A faint light was just beginning to glow on the far side of the city; it would soon be day. As much as she wanted to gallop headlong into the city in broad daylight, yelping as loudly as she could for Scruff, she knew she'd be better off finding some food and getting some rest before continuing under darkness.

The day felt torturously long. She found some wild blueberries and killed a few hours snacking. When she smelled a large animal coming — thankfully not a monster cat — she descended the edge of the plateau, drawing close to the first few houses and hoping to find safety there. She spent the last few hours before sunset curled up under a large tree, trying and failing to sleep. When darkness finally fell, she rose to her feet, exhaustion and electric excitement mixing together in her body. She was both numb and tingly. As she walked, she had to look down to make sure her legs were still there.

Sticking to the shadows, she wound her way along the dark neighbourhood roads. She headed for the smell of the ocean, a familiar landmark. At first, she wasn't sure if she was entering the city or the Wild Lands. She shivered, flashbacks of the dangerous crossing from the city to the Wild Lands filling her with dread. Would she have to make that crossing again?

A few minutes later, her heart jumped. Her first landmark was a large parking lot that was almost empty. She clearly remembered the night they had found this parking lot. They had just arrived, hungry and cold, and were looking for mice around the oversized garbage bins when a freezing rain started up. The wind had blown the rain sideways, driving the small needles of ice through their fur into their tender skin. They had leapt under a truck for cover and curled up around each other, shivering.

"Great spot," Scruff had said dryly. Pica had started laughing, then Scruff, and the two of them had not stopped for the next few minutes. Pica hadn't even known what was so funny, but at that point, laughing was better than crying.

Tonight, only a soft breeze ruffled Pica's fur. A lifetime had passed since that night. Shaking her head, she skirted the parking lot and continued on, now orienting herself toward the power lines. The smells and the sounds of the Wild Lands were so familiar that emotion welled up in her throat, choking her. The oily smell of pavement mixed with the soft smells of human food. In the distance, car tires thrummed along busy roads. The clouds glowed with the reflection of lights from thousands of houses. Here, there was always some kind of action, be it night or day. She was far away from the dark, still lands of the last few months. Breathing deeply, she allowed hope to carry her faster.

Just before dawn, she reached the rows of houses closest to the power lines. Slowing down, she carefully sniffed each pole and bush, looking for traces of Scruff and leaving her scent behind to let him know she'd been there. With each step, disappointment grew. There were no signs of Scruff. Still, she had to see for herself.

She skirted a skinny, dark house and squeezed under its backyard fence into the scrubby green space that ran behind the houses. Power lines criss-crossed above her head, dark against the glowing clouds. A few more steps, and she was standing in front of the bushes where she had rested after the monster cat attack. Her heart fell. She didn't have to sniff around to know that Scruff wasn't here, and he hadn't been here for a long time. She smelled another coyote who had passed through recently, and she stumbled across a family of raccoons, but there was definitely no trace of Scruff, and no clue as to where he had gone.

She steadied her breath. She was strong, and she knew the Wild Lands well. If he was still here, she would find him.

Over the next few days, Pica exhausted herself combing the Wild Lands in search of Scruff. The Wild Lands stretched for a long distance beyond what they had explored together, so she made sure to scour each section, neighbourhood by neighbourhood. Some areas she didn't enter, being run off by a particularly aggressive coyote pack or unable to cross a highway. However, she felt certain that if Scruff was still living somewhere in the Wild Lands, and if she left a wide radius of scent, he would eventually come across it, so she focused on making large circles through every area.

One night, she came across a smell that stopped her in her tracks. She was in familiar territory, following the train tracks not far from the ocean. She bent down to sniff the base of a signpost and caught the unmistakable odour of Jagger. Her head whipped up and she looked around, suddenly very alert. The smell was fresh. She crouched, ready to run, still scanning the area. Nothing. Her mind spun. What was Jagger doing here? Why would he have crossed into the Wild Lands, too? Whatever the reason, she didn't want to stay here another moment. She fled, following the train tracks until she found a good exit into the safety of a neighbourhood. She would not go there again. And if Jagger was there, it definitely wasn't an area where Scruff would be. She would give that place a wide berth from here on out.

Weeks passed. Pica was happy to discover that the better weather meant more available food. Not enough to feel full, but enough to keep up her energy for the search. The Wild Lands had transformed while she'd been away. Now there were backyards filled with berry bushes, human leftovers spilling from the park garbage bins, and more insects, frogs, and snakes. With her bad paw, she didn't catch any rodents, but she ate more than enough to be able to keep looking for Scruff.

However, with each day, Pica's hope diminished. There was no sign of Scruff anywhere in the Wild Lands.

She had been gone for almost two seasons. It was looking more and more like Scruff had moved on. Maybe he had found a new pack or struck out in a new direction. She had no idea where he was, but she was beginning to feel sure that he was not in the Wild Lands anymore.

One hot day, curled up under a bush just to the side of a busy street, she forced herself to consider what to do next. With her injured paw and her small size, she had very little chance of intimidating other coyotes. She wouldn't be able to make a home here without the constant threat of losing it. And if she stayed too long looking, it would be winter again. That thought filled her with dread.

By night, she'd figured out what she needed to do. She dragged her tired, sad body through the Wild Lands, aiming for the water. Once there, she picked her way along the railroad tracks. The bridge loomed ahead of her against the night sky. As much as she dreaded leaving this place and abandoning any hope of ever seeing Scruff again, she knew her only hope of survival was to find her family again while the weather was still good. Her mother, Gree, would happily take her in again, and she would be protected once more.

TWENTY-FIVE
SCENT

Scruff

As spring turned into summer, Scruff had felt a restlessness visit him each night. At first, he'd been happy to find food in the small area around the ravine, thankful to have a home and not worry about other coyotes or strange, unexpected dangers. But after a while, the days and nights felt long and slow, and he began exploring farther away from the ravine, just for something to do.

Tonight, he felt drawn to the water. He found a deserted beach and lay down on the sand, which was still warm from the day. The waves lapped the shore gently, and he breathed in rhythm with it, the night noises surrounding him.

After a few hours, he grew bored and picked his way along the water, looking for food. As he arrived at the base of the large bridge, memories of Pica stirred inside him. Even at night, a steady stream of cars and trucks passed overhead. His paws felt the steady vibrations in the earth. A lifetime ago, he had arrived on this bridge with Pica, ready to start a new life.

With a sigh, he stopped to sniff one of the tall metal pillars that stretched up to support the wide bridge deck. He frowned and sniffed again. Yes, he was absolutely sure. Pica had been here, and not long ago!

Lifting his head, he howled into the night. If she was close, he had to find her. He couldn't lose this lead. He waited and listened. Nothing but the cars racing above him. They were so loud — maybe she couldn't hear him. He raced a few blocks away from the noisy bridge and tried another howl. Still nothing. Crossing back under the bridge, he tried again from the other side. And then, clear and pure, just audible over the sound of the traffic, came a reply.

He careened toward the sound, yipping as he ran. He followed the human path that went along the edge of the water, scanning the area ahead of him and stopping to listen every minute or so. He turned a corner — and there she was. Her unmistakable profile, with one paw in the air.

"Pica!" he yelped, running headlong into her and knocking her over.

"Scruff!" she said in a sob.

"Where did you … what … how …?" His thoughts ran into each other so that he couldn't even form a question. He searched her face for answers.

"I almost didn't make it," she said, her eyes haunted. "I almost didn't make it back to you."

His heart clenched. "Pica, I'm so sorry. For whatever I said in the fight. I didn't mean to make you run away."

"I didn't run away."

"You didn't?"

She sighed. "I have so much to tell you. I don't even know where to start."

Scruff nodded. "Let's find somewhere safer to talk. I have a lot to tell you, too."

Pica led the way, and he followed her. Noticing that she wasn't putting weight on one of her paws, his eyes widened. What had happened to her?

A few moments later, curled up against a brick wall in the shelter of a large tree, she began. In a halting voice raspy with emotion, she related trial after trial, from getting locked in a truck, to being hunted by wolves, then getting caught in a leg trap, being rescued by a coyote pack, and finally making the long journey back. He didn't interrupt, although it was hard for him to even imagine some of the things she was talking about. He knew there would be time for questions later.

"I knew you'd think I ran away because I was mad. I was so worried that …" She stopped.

"That I would be with a new family?"

"Yes." She glanced at him shyly. "Are you? What have you been doing since I left? Why couldn't I find you anywhere?"

Scruff opened his mouth to answer, then shut it. How was he going to tell her about Jagger? He launched into his story slowly, giving himself time to figure out his words. He told her about Kaia and her pack, though he stopped short of explaining how close they had become, instead saying they'd all become friends. He returned to the truth to describe Kaia and Casper's death in detail. "I know now just how dangerous humans are. I had no idea before. You were right. We should never go near them if we don't have to."

Pica blinked a few times. "Humans are dangerous, but stealing some of their food a few times was what helped me to get back to you. I think the problem of humans is more complicated than either of us knew when we fought about that bread truck."

There was a silence as they both digested this. Then Pica cocked her head to the side to study Scruff. "So, what did you do after she died?"

Scruff couldn't avoid it any longer. "I was very afraid of humans for a long time. Still am, I guess. I was feeling so lost. I'd almost given up on everything, but then someone gave me a place to live. It's where I'm living now. A good place. Safe. You're probably not going to like this, but please, hear me out."

Pica shut her eyes and dipped her head, steadying her breath like she was ready for bad news. "Okay, you can tell me. I know I was gone a long time. I understand why you ended up finding a new family."

"No, Pica, I don't think you do. It's Jagger. I'm living with Jagger."

"What?" she yelped, the loudest sound she'd made since Scruff found her.

"It's complicated. You said you would listen."

She narrowed her eyes. "Fine."

"I was lonely and depressed. He offered me a place to live and be safe, with no strings attached. He also told me about my family and how he ended up in the forest beside your family's golf course. He was driven out by our parents when he was still a pup. He had to figure out how to fend for himself without any help from anyone. He's had a hard life. I'll never forgive him for it, but I understand a bit better now why he did what he did. He was scared of losing his way of life. Just like your family was when they drove my parents away. Coyote life can be violent, and much as I don't like it, each of our families was just trying to protect their own."

Pica sighed, emotions flying across her face. "I hear what you're saying, and it is sad. But he lied to you, and he threatened us. He's not an honourable coyote. He's not only violent, he's manipulative, too."

"I've been with him for a few months now. He doesn't try to manipulate me anymore. He doesn't say much, but he gives me more respect now that I'm not dependent on him." Scruff took a shaky breath. "He's my brother. Other than you, he's the only one in the world who cares about me. And the part I really wanted to tell you is that he and I have a good territory. A home. A place where we could survive next winter together. Please, just come and talk to him."

"No."

"Well, where else are we going to go? You've only got three good legs, you're far too skinny. You need a few months to get stronger, and we need a safe place to live. It's messy, but it would give us time. We can use the ravine as a base while we continue looking for our own home."

She stared back at him angrily. "I don't trust him. Why is he helping you now, all of a sudden? How do you know he isn't just doing it for his own benefit?"

"Pica, he's my brother."

"That's not enough."

"Why are you making me choose?"

"The choice should be easier."

Scruff huffed in frustration. He couldn't believe that moments after being reunited, they were fighting again. He breathed in deeply. "Fine. You don't have to trust him. But we can still stay there while we figure out what to do. I'm proud of you for being strong enough to survive that journey, but I can see that it's taken a toll on you. Let's take a few weeks to catch up, to be safe, and to fatten up. As soon as you're healthier, we can leave."

Pica sighed again. Her eyes softened. "Okay. I trust *you*. I'll go and meet him. But if he threatens me, I'm gone."

TWENTY-SIX
HOME

Scruff

They made their way along the railroad tracks back to
Jagger's ravine. Pica moved slowly, but Scruff was surprised at how well she balanced, considering she was only
putting full weight on three of her paws. He suspected
that she was moving slowly more because of Jagger than
because of her injury. He shuddered, picturing the sharp
metal jaws that had snapped shut on her paw. From her
story, it sounded like life wasn't any easier outside the city
and the Wild Lands.

"Was it weird to come back here after getting used to
living with only grass and sticks?" Scruff asked as they
crossed a busy road.

Pica looked back and wrinkled her nose at him. "No, it felt like coming home."

They continued on companionably, but as they approached the ravine, Scruff could see Pica's body stiffening. Finally, she stopped. "I don't know if I can do this."

Scruff knew he couldn't push her. There was still time before daybreak, so he changed direction and guided them down a steep alley toward a series of tall houses. He led her through a hole in the hedge into a huge backyard filled with towering cedar trees. The house was dark and still.

"It's beautiful here," Pica breathed.

"I only come here in the middle of the night, but I love it."

The grass was cool on their paws as they explored the yard, digging for slugs in the soft soil of the garden and nibbling the tender plants that grew there. Scruff wanted to talk some more, but couldn't find a way to start. Pica lay down with a sigh under one of the sentinel trees. He lay down beside her, feeling the warmth of her body against his. It felt strange and familiar at the same time.

Suddenly, there was a loud *pssshh*, and water shot into the air from various points across the lawn. Scruff had seen this before, but Pica jumped up, her body shaking. Seeing his calmness, she frowned, then looked back at the water streaming in large arcs across the lawn.

"What is it?"

"I'm not sure. The water comes on and sprays all the grass, then later, it just goes off." He smiled. "All right, wolf fighter. Let's see how brave you really are!" He crouched low, wiggling his hind legs, then leapt up and raced straight through the first jet of water. It hit him square on, parting his fur and stinging his skin with its pressure and coldness. He looked behind him to see an expression he knew well — Pica was not about to let a challenge go unmet.

She followed his footsteps, yelping when the water hit her. She danced to the side and out of the way, shaking out her fur. "What was that?" She cried out, shaking her head. "You call that fun?"

"It is fun!"

"If you like hurting yourself."

"Well, it's not gentle," he laughed. "But how do you feel now?"

She stood tall, her thick fur dripping and shining. Scruff had forgotten how beautiful she was. "Wow. I feel wonderful. I feel like I suddenly have more energy."

"Right?" With a small smile, he suggested, "Again?"

"Okay, you're officially crazy. I feel good. I'm going to leave it at that."

Laughing, he ran through the water one more time before joining her closer to the house, where water was pooling on the concrete. Drinking deeply next to her, he sighed. He had missed her so much. It hurt him to think of everything she had gone through to get back to him. And the whole time, he'd thought she had left him on purpose. The words she had spoken earlier echoed in his head: "I trust you." She had never lost faith in him. He, on the other hand, had found another pack. He shuddered to think what would have happened if he'd still been with Kaia when Pica had come back. He resolved to do everything he could to honour the trust she placed in him. It was a gift.

They finished drinking, and as they went back out to the street, he sensed a new calm in Pica. Without speaking, they headed for the ravine.

Pica

She had put it off as long as she could. Dawn was breaking, and house lights were popping on everywhere. Garage doors were opening and cars were slipping out onto the roads. It was time.

As they approached, she began to smell Jagger's territory markings, and her eyes darted around warily. The last time she'd seen Jagger, he'd attacked her. She couldn't believe that he'd changed, or that he'd simply been misunderstood before. Scruff was right, though. It would be helpful to have a home base while they figured out what to do next.

She followed Scruff down a steep embankment, slipping down the loose dirt. As she reached the bottom, Jagger stood up from behind a bush, his lean, grey form looking much stronger than it had the last time she had seen him. Despite her exhaustion, she drew herself up to her maximum height and puffed out her chest.

"Pica, what a surprise." Jagger raised his eyebrows in an unspoken question. Pica watched as he and Scruff touched noses gently, noting how close they had become.

She couldn't quite bring herself to touch his nose, but she did walk closer and wag her tail a few times to show her good faith.

"Hello, Jagger."

An awkward silence followed. Scruff flicked his eyes back and forth from Jagger to Pica.

"Scruff told me you'd left."

Pica narrowed her eyes and turned to Scruff, who looked uncomfortable now. "What?"

"I didn't tell him what happened between us. Just that you left."

Jagger laughed. "He said it didn't work out, so you went your separate ways. But I guess you're back."

Scruff wouldn't meet Pica's eyes for a moment, then he looked up, pained. "I didn't want to tell Jagger what happened between us, so I just said it didn't work out. I didn't want to seem weak, I guess. I thought you'd left on purpose."

"You really thought I'd leave you over a stupid fight?" Even though Pica could understand why he had thought this, part of her still felt hurt that he had. "With Kaia, were you really just hanging out? Or were you starting a pack with her?"

Scruff looked down. Pica looked from Scruff to Jagger, who had an amused expression on his face. And again, even though she had prepared herself for the possibility of Scruff moving on without her, anger licked up through her body. She spun around and headed back up the embankment.

"Pica, wait!" Scruff called out.

She didn't look back. She didn't want to see the hurt in his face.

She wove through the neighbourhood until she found a clump of bushes at the front of a random house. She sniffed carefully — no dogs. In the dawn light, it was probably as far as she was going to get. She crawled underneath the bushes to a hollow in the middle and lay down. Her mind swirled. How had Scruff given up on her so easily? She felt betrayed and humiliated in front of Jagger. Her head throbbed.

Moments later, she sensed Scruff approaching. She didn't move, but heard his sniffing getting closer and closer, until his little black nose poked through the bush.

"Pica?" he began hesitantly. "Can I please join you?"

"Okay."

He squeezed in beside her and lay down, not quite touching her. Warmth radiated in the small space between them. She couldn't quite bring herself to look at him.

He began right away. "You're right. About everything. I did try to move on. I'm sorry that I thought you would leave like that without coming back to talk about it. I feel terrible that I didn't have faith in you. I'm also sorry that I lied to Jagger. I don't know what I was thinking."

"I'm so angry at you." Pica tried to find a clear, honest way to share what she was feeling. "But I guess I'm less angry that you gave up on me and more that you didn't tell me the whole truth tonight. To find that out from Jagger — it was humiliating."

Scruff was silent for a moment. "I wish we were back in the forest together, running from that cat. The things we were up against were so simple. Food. Shelter. I wish I could undo all the terrible things that have happened to us."

"I wish we were back there, too."

"Listen, Pica. I don't know how, but I'm going to make it up to you and prove that you can trust me. We can leave, go back to the city. I'll even take you home to your family, if that's what you want. But let me help you."

Pica shifted slightly and closed the gap between their bodies. Feeling his soft fur brush hers, her breathing deepened. Scruff had always had a calming effect on her, and she had really missed him.

"Okay."

"Okay?"

"I'll stay with you in Jagger's territory until I'm stronger. I still don't trust him, and I don't understand why you do. But I don't want to go off on my own or go back to my family without you. For me, home isn't just a place. It's you, Scruff. You are my home."

Scruff leaned into her, and his breathing slowed to match hers. A warm contentment flooded through her.

Later, when darkness returned, they padded back to the ravine. Pica stifled the tension that welled up in her as soon as she saw Jagger. If nothing else, he was Scruff's brother, and he had helped Scruff when no one else would. She would have to trust Jagger long enough for her to get strong again. She took a deep breath.

"Hi, Jagger."

He stood to greet her, his tail wagging slowly. "Hi, Pica. You've come back."

"I was hoping to stay here with you two for a little while."

Jagger looked at her, then at Scruff, then back at her. He nodded. "Of course."

"Thank you."

After another awkward pause, Jagger turned and went to lie down on the far side of the ravine. Pica hesitated, not knowing what to do. Scruff touched her nose with his.

"You okay?"

Pica sighed. "I think so. It kind of feels like a dream to be standing here with you, you know? I didn't think I'd ever see you again." She shook her head. "And I never thought I'd see Jagger again."

Scruff moved closer to her and laid his head gently on her back, letting the gurgling creek do the talking. Pica relaxed into being with her best friend again. Despite everything, she did feel like she was finally home.

The peace of the moment was broken by a loud grumble from her stomach. Scruff's head whipped up. "That almost sounded like a monster cat!" he said, grinning.

Pica groaned. "Don't remind me."

Scruff shook out his fur. "Do you want to come hunting with me?"

Pica narrowed her eyes, staring him down. "No human food?"

Scruff shook his head and looked her straight in the eye. "From here on out, I'm going to stay as far from humans as I can get. There's a great hunting spot by the railroad tracks we can go to."

Pica smiled. "Sounds like it's time to meet the local mice."

Scruff led the way up and out of the ravine. When they reached flat ground, Pica fell in step beside him. A thin veil of cloud covered the moon, and the cool night air cleared her head. She let go of all her heavy thoughts and turned her attention to the feeling of rough pavement under her paws, the smells left behind from the day, and the sound of distant cars moving through the night. Finally, she was exactly where she needed to be.

The two coyotes' footsteps fell into a single rhythm, and they moved along fluidly, a single shadow in the night.

DID YOU KNOW?

1. **Homing instincts are real.** When Pica is trying to figure out how to get home, her gut feeling about direction is real! Many animals have incredible homing skills, or the ability to return home after being displaced from it. Some well-known examples are birds and fish, but homing skills have also been documented in larger animals such as deer, bears, and coyotes. One review by the U.S. Forest Service in Minnesota listed a study where a deer travelled 560 kilometres to make its way home!

2. **Coyotes and badgers do actually hunt together.** According to the U.S. Fish and Wildlife Service, coyotes and badgers are known to team up and hunt together, just like Scruff and Bodi. The coyote can chase

down prey if it runs, and the badger is an excellent digger if the prey heads underground. In 2020, a video taken in San Francisco showed a coyote and a badger travelling together under a highway in the middle of the night. (youtu.be/mGyHlYPupHg)

3. **There's no evidence of a coyote ever having been transported by a delivery truck, but they have been seen on other modes of transportation**. One high-profile story in *National Geographic* featured a coyote who, in 2002, hopped on the light rail from the airport in Portland and got comfortable on a seat. (nationalgeographic.com/news/2013/4/130424-animals-weird-cats-science-world-trains-buses/)

4. **Leg-hold traps are real, and they are still legal in almost every province of Canada and state of the United States.** These traps are extremely traumatic and painful for the animals, who mostly die from hypothermia, thirst, or blood loss. Some animals resort to chewing off their own trapped limbs in the process of trying to escape. Many groups oppose leg traps, including the Sierra Club, the American Animal Hospital Association, and the National Animal Care & Control Association.

5. **Coyotes strongly prefer eating rodents and plants to human garbage.** Many researchers, including Stan Gehrt (2007) and Victoria Lukasik and Shelley Alexander (2012), have pointed out that human sources

of food typically only make up about 5 to 15 percent of coyote diets. However, when humans make food available to coyotes, even in an effort to help, it inevitably hurts the coyotes. Coyotes fed by humans are much more likely to become lazy and to associate food with humans. They will gravitate to where the food is, putting them in conflict with other humans. Often, such coyotes are deemed a "problem" and have to be killed.

6. **Coyotes help each other when they are injured.** Several coyotes in this story need help from other coyotes, either for food or to fend off potential hazards. This type of altruistic behaviour has been observed by Janet Kessler in San Francisco in her blog, *Coyote Yipps*. For example, one coyote led dogs away from her injured mate, risking her own safety to make sure that he could continue to rest.

ACKNOWLEDGEMENTS

My own love and passion can only take my stories so far. From there, I rely on a talented and dedicated team of people to help me transform a somewhat readable story into the novel you are reading today. The following people are part of this team, and I would like to extend my warmest appreciation for the part that each of them has played.

Scott Fraser and the rest of the team at Dundurn Press supported the continuation of Pica and Scruff's story. In particular, Kathryn Lane, associate publisher at Dundurn Press, took time out of her busy pandemic life to understand the potential of this story and to champion it. Susan Fitzgerald gave me the most comprehensive and helpful editing notes I have ever received. Catharine Chen's copy edit suggestions were thorough and greatly improved the action scenes. Laura Boyle once again designed a perfect cover the first time around. Barbara Bradford and Janet Kessler took the time to pore over early versions of this story and provide expert feedback.

Ultimately, though, none of these people would have even seen a manuscript if it hadn't been for the support of my family. Finishing a novel while teaching full-time and raising a family is not for the faint of heart. My deepest love and thanks go out to Seth for helping me carve out writing time, to Zoe for happily watching *Paw Patrol* so I could edit, and to all of my American and Canadian friends and family for their constant support and encouragement. "I couldn't have done it without you" may be a trite statement, but in this case, it is absolutely true.

ABOUT THE AUTHOR

Claire Gilchrist got the inspiration to write about coyotes when she and her dog were chased through a graveyard one night in Vancouver, B.C., by a scary grey shape. Although at first she was sure it was a ghost, she realized quickly that it was a coyote who was most likely defending new pups from the threat of her dog. This moment sparked years of research and imagination, leading to the creation of the Song Dog series. In addition to coyotes, Claire also loves hummingbirds, bats, and mountain lions, and hopes to share these interests with her two daughters as they grow older.

READ THE FIRST
SONG DOG ADVENTURE!

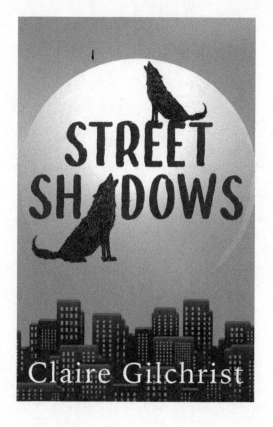

Teacher's Resource Guides available
at dundurn.com/resources.